Beneath the Floating City

And other science fiction short stories

By

Donna Maree Hanson

Note: The author uses Australian/British spelling conventions.

Copyright Information
First published by Aust Spec Fiction (Donna Maree Hanson) in 2017.

Copyright © Donna Maree Hanson 2017.
Beneath the Floating City: and other science fiction short stories

This is the first publication of 'Lake Absence'. All other stories in this collection have been published previously.

CIP National Library of Australia
Ebook ISBN 978-0-6480650-8-1
Print version published 2018
Print ISBN 978-0-6482795-0-1

Cover art by Patty Jansen http://pattyjansen.com

Contents

Beneath the Floating City

The flashing lights and the easy stride of narcotics through his system kept Nic Da Silva gyrating on the dance floor. The low hum of voices of the club patrons combined with the drumming beat of the dance music flowed over him. Nic grinned as the woman dancing with him tucked a wad of credits into the front of his trousers, her hand dropping slightly, stroking him, lingering there possessive, slightly aggressive. It was enough money to pay his shot at the inn for another night. God how he loved Hedonia.

'Let's leave now, Mr Engineer,' the woman whispered in his ear, her breath a warm, spicy tickle. 'My hotel is across the road.' Nic nodded and he followed the woman out, her body draped in translucent robes that shifted and swayed with as she walked. At least he thought she was a woman, a human woman. There was so much enhancement these days it was hard to tell. The Club Zephyr was patronised by humans mostly but that didn't mean other races didn't try their luck. Exotic, erotic encounters. He shrugged mentally. As long as there was mutual satisfaction and, as she'd paid, he'd do the necessary no matter what the removal of her clothes revealed. A few scales, an excess of mucous hadn't put him off before. A man's gotta eat.

A city engineer leaning against the bar caught his eye and winked as Nic passed through the main doors. Engineers on Hedonia were a bunch of stuck up bastards, if he had ever met any. He'd been trying to get into that profession for so long that he'd gotten used to being invisible to that lot at the club. Nic saluted in a casual way, acknowledging the man. Another engineer joined him and they both turned their backs. Still, Nic was heartened by

1

the attention, a friendly wink was better than a punch in the nose. Their presence was why he frequented that particular club. He was an engineer, too, by profession, but unemployed, recently retrenched from the mines on Xeno. His severance pay had got him to Hedonia, it was up to him to do the rest. Hedonia, the decadent floating city, a holiday haven for those with money and the will to spend it, with little to show in the end but a blur of a narcotic haze, zero remaining credit and maybe a sexually transmitted disease or three.

Lucky for him this is where he wanted to be for the present and damn if he wasn't going to have a good time while he eked out an existence, sleeping in third grade hotels, slumming it in bars and earning his way with his other great organ. In his current state of mind, decadence was good for the soul. Being an engineer certainly helped, but he was not a Hedonian City engineer. They had status because of the great marvel of the place and the secrecy behind the tech, while he had no status. Zilch.

The woman he accompanied waved her ID card at the monitor and the doors to the hotel swished open. Not bad, he thought, as they walked through the plush surroundings. Everything had been done to augment the ancient alien design of the building, even the air was slightly green-tinged. Richly carved stone walls, full with alien figures doing what came naturally complete with patterned borders full of swirls and interlinking designs. Once in the elevator the woman pushed him back against the wall and groped him, making him grunt in surprise.

'My, you're hot tonight, pretty lady,' he said in his best gigolo voice. She purred as she rubbed herself against him, so maybe his charm had worked already.

The lift door opened to her suite. They tumbled inside, kissing up a frenzy and the lights went on.

2

'Take them off,' she said pulling back, her own fingers separating the robe she was wearing. Yellow, it spilt like sunburst and landed in a delicate puddle on the floor.

Nic paused. The woman was stunning. Firm breasts with brown nut nipples, great tan, long lean thighs. He realised he was standing half naked with his mouth opened and shut it. Why did this woman need a paid fuck? You'd think she'd have to fight them off, the men wanting to pay her for her time and not the other way around. Their bodies crashed together. The room lurched around him as he found himself held firmly, face down on the floor, arm twisted up his back. 'What the—'

**

Next morning, Nic's eyes were gooey and his nose was filled with a particularly nasty stench. Waking up proved to him that he had indeed been thrown out of the hotel, according the door receipt he held in his hand, exactly one hour and thirty four minutes after he had arrived. Groaning he levered himself up on his elbows. He was in the gutter. Figures. Blasted trans, can't trust them as far as you can root them. Of course its body had been too good to be true. It was a transmuter alien, able to morph sex, shape its body into other species, appearing anyway it chose. It had fucked him senseless taking it every way and then some, then sucked out all his brain juice. That's when it started getting kinky. Staggering to his feet, he felt a wave of exhaustion hit him. A needle headache shot through his skull. 'Argh!' he blurted, unable to hold it in. Squinting, he realised he was a block or two from his own flop house. He could make it there, maybe they'd even let him sleep in a bed all day. He checked his pants. At least the cash was still there.

It took a while to get into his room. He had to pay first and negotiate the next payment. He used the san unit, the harsh jets washing the street scum and transmuter juice off him. He thwacked the wall in frustration. No wonder the blasted engineer acknowledged him on the way out. All this time wasted trying to fraternise with them, trying to wheedle his way into a job and the bastards were laughing at him. He'd rooted alien arse. Shit! He had his own penetrated as well as the mental shakedown. What a rape of the mind that was. The creature got high on his emotions, his memories and thoughts. Nothing was secret now. When it realised what he was, what he was after, it had laughed and thrown him out. Real bone fide, licensed gigolos had more interesting minds than an out of work engineer and better sense than to mess with transmuters in the first place.

Though his mind felt rather empty when he woke up, he thought there was no permanent harm done. The thrill for the transmuter in sucking brain was in the taking, in the struggle and the pain inflicted as the thoughts were ripped out.

Later, Nic half limped to the Zephyr Club, expecting that none of the engineers would be there. It was midday and already the place was filling up. A few new shuttles had arrived and the tourists didn't let city time interfere with their visit. Hedonia was a place of indulgence after all—an ancient and alien floating city, full of aged opulence and mysterious technology.

The tourists in the club were a mixed bag of those who had been in the city for a couple of days to those who had recently arrived. The older ones could be distinguished by the jaded, slightly greasy skin tone as something in the atmosphere created an unnatural sheen to human skin. As no ill effects had been experienced, except the

4

discolouration, scientists had put it down to a type of local fungi. Nic's own swarthy complexion had deepened to a golden brown. He liked the shine.

He was on his second drink and feeling mellow when the engineer he'd been waiting for arrived. Quite blithely, the man fronted up to him and slapped him on the shoulder. 'So how was it?' he asked with a grin.

'Bleeding bastard. You could have warned me it was a transmuter. My head hurts still.' So did his rear but he wasn't owning to that.

The engineer nodded. 'Better you experience the brain drain now while you still know nothing. We suspect they are after the specs for the floatation engines.'

'Fat lot of good it does me. Can't even get an interview with you lot.'

The man grinned and waved to the barkeep. 'As it happens there is an opening. There's a workbus leaving in two hours for an undercity inspection. If you are interested, make sure your credentials have been lodged with the city. There'll be a test afterward. Tell them, Johann sent you. The foreman's a Fleche so don't wear any colognes or strong scents. It overwhelms his olfactory senses and makes him twice as cranky as he normally is.'

Johann turned away, slapping his business card on the counter as he did. Nic gaped at it stupidly, not quite believing his luck. If he sealed this deal, he'd be legit, a resident and also in funds. A whole pathway of future plans opened up to him.

Without finishing his drink, he pushed away from the bar and ignored the sexual overtures of two over eroticised bi-pedal females. Next time he slapped his flesh against a woman, it would be because he wanted to, not because he was desperate for money. Glancing over his shoulder at the second woman, a Taelen, he saw she wasn't too bad. With a shrug, he decided to trust to luck that they'd cross paths again and he'd be in the mood.

***

There were nine other contenders for the one vacant position. Nic ground his teeth as he attempted to assess the competition. The Fleche was giving nothing away, not even a twitch of his elephantine nose, which looked more a like a penis than a nose. Nic tried not to think of the noun 'fuckface' or 'dickhead' when he looked at him, because he knew he'd start to laugh. He turned away to order his thoughts in a more professional manner.

The twelve seater workbus took off from a service dock, quickly rising over the city. In this sector, some of the ancient buildings appeared to be sinking. He wondered how the buildings remained upright as some had a serious tilt. The buildings looked to be made of stone, covered over with the same greasy gold sheen as the people of Hedonia eventually acquired. Nic rubbed his chin, feeling the slight layer of film on his chin, even his tongue had acquired the colour, though it was more brown than gold.

Ornate arched bridges linked sections of the city, spanning nothing at all except the plummeting depths of the atmosphere to the surface below. As the workbus pivoted over the perimeter of the city, Nic held his breath, getting his first look at the colossal engines holding it up.

Underneath the floating city huge turbines larger than the buildings they supported whirred and droned. Enough thrust to keep the city afloat and enough momentum to keep it fairly still. It wasn't truly stationary, but the tether meant it floated in a slow arc. Any movement the city made was undetectable to the inhabitants. The physics of it blew Nic's mind. So much so that his head ached sharply and then eased, leaving him feeling queasy.

Housing the turbines were fluted pillars ending in ornate grapples, clutching the machine housing. Never had Nic seen anything so beautiful and mysterious. Over the loudspeaker, the Fleche explained the purpose of the turbines, obvious thought Nic, but he listened anyway in case the test at the end included some idiosyncratic commentary from the foreman. Nic noticed that what the foreman said was veiled to hide the true properties of the alien technology. Any engineer worth his salt could at least map out what was being done, the difficultly lay in the how.

Further in, he glimpsed walkways and cathedral style doors, disguising sufficient space to accommodate thousands. He figured that the builders of the place must have lived beneath the city as well as on the top. The Lynex race, the name bestowed on the builders of the city, had disappeared long before humans and other species had come to this sector. Carved images, thought to be depictions of the Lynex, were spread through the buildings and some of those images implied that the city was a place of decadence and indulgence for them too. To a human eye, they were downright erotic in places. His gaze once again went to the gantries and those closed doors. What secrets did those passageways contain?

'Excuse me,' Nic asked the foreman, pointing. 'Those walkways and passageways. Are they used by the workcrews?'

The Fleche's nose twitched. 'At times is it necessary to access them. Most are sealed by order of the city council.'

'Sealed? Why?'

'The city council do not explain themselves to their employees. We have extrapolated their reasoning to determine that safety concerns are at the forefront of the edict. There is also a seal on most corridors placed by the

Academy of Exoscience that is currently undertaking research.'

'So what happens if you need to gain access to repair a turbine or perform maintenance?'

'We use work harnesses. Only if the machinery is inaccessible by this means do we request access.'

Nic swallowed. The workbus was sealed but outside the wind was cold and powerful. A man wouldn't survive long in a workharness and, if suited, then dexterity would be inhibited. There must be something worth hiding if the engineers were forced to those extremes.

The workbus finished its inspection of the undercity and returned to the dock. The Fleche led them to a small room with info-terminals at the ready. 'You will take a seat and sit the test. Please register your ID and commence.'

Nic waved his ID card and the first test question flashed up. It was a fairly basic equation. The next question related to a piece of commentary from the tour, the next a bit of detail from the turbines that he happened to pick up on. Then the questions got harder. He had no idea how long the test took because the Fleche called to a halt and the terminal screens froze. Nic had no idea even if he had finished the test. Surprisingly, he answered the questions readily, despite having his brain drained less than twenty four hours previously.

'You will be notified of the outcome within twenty four hours.' Nic nodded and left the room. Man he needed a drink or a Tee, so he headed back to the Zephyr Club, hoping that he'd showed the right stuff and landed the job. When he entered the bar, the engineers gathered by the bar welcomed him and Johann slapped him on the back. 'So how did you go?'

'Good, I think. Beneath the city was fascinating. My head is full of it, full of the possibilities.'

Johann smiled. 'Yep it was like that for me too. So are you selling your body tonight or drinking with us?'

Nic's eyes widened and then he nodded. He hoped the golden tinge to his skin hid his blush. 'With you, of course!'

The bastards knew what he been doing all these weeks. Knew and did nothing to help. Like to see them down on their luck and see how they like it. Nic got wasted that night. He wasn't sure how he made it back to his hotel, but he did and woke up alone.

At reception, he found a sealed package in his secure niche, along with the bill for the next night's accommodation. He ripped package open to find an acceptance letter, employment details, including salary, fraternization restrictions and confidentiality agreements and the news that he had to report at his assigned dormitory that evening. As he read all the conditions of his employment over a hot coffee in the hotel annexe, he realised his foray into the high life would now be curtailed. He could go to the assigned bar but had a curfew, and had to sleep in his assigned quarters, no visitors allowed. That's why the engineers were so standoffish. It was part of their job description. He recalled how he had blundered in there, asking questions up front about the turbines, about the aeolus gas and its properties. No wonder the bastards had shunned him all that time.

Returning to his room, he gathered up his gear and had it sent to his new accommodation. Then he checked out, paying the last of the bill with the money he had remaining. He hoped food came with the accommodation or he'd be mighty hungry before payday.

Back at the Zephyr he nursed his drink, taking it slowly as he had no cash for another. The engineers dribbled in groups of twos and threes after their shift. There was only about fifteen of them who were regulars.

Johann sidled up to him. 'I hear congratulations are in order. Buy you a drink?'

'Thanks. Thanks for the tip too. Appreciate it. I'll take a drink but I can't repay the favour until payday.'

'No more tricks from now on, heh? Man, how I hated that when I came here.'

Taking a sip of his drink, Nic nearly choked. As it was, he sprayed beer over the bar in a wide spray. 'You did what?'

'Same as you. Not much else to do around here unless you want to turn narc dealer. Lucky for me it only took me two weeks to get a place.'

Nic gaped at Johann. 'So are there vacancies because the engineers leave or is there more and more work opening up?'

Johann shook his head. 'A bit of both, except they disappear or die but I guess you call that leaving permanently.'

Nic took the new drink the bartender handed him. It was spicy and warm just how he liked his brew. 'Disappear? Die? How?' He thought about the workharnesses and how difficult the work would be, perilous too if you weren't careful. Surely the city would protect their workers. There were a lot of engineers around but still, recruitment costs, benefits.

Johann took a long draw on his beer, closing his eyes. 'Different ways I suppose.'

Nic frowned into his glass. He wasn't stupid. He knew hedging when he saw it. 'So are you warning me, giving me safety tips? I want to live, for a very long time actually.'

'Neither. I've been working here three years now. I haven't had any problems myself. But you hear stuff, you know.'

'Yes I do.'

They finished their drink making idle talk with the others who joined them. Mostly they watched the dancers, the tourist drunk on vacation, narcs and sex. He watched them, like the engineers had watched him. Quite a sobering thought. Before midnight the engineers began to drift out the door. Johann led him to the street. 'I'll show you to your new home. Your room is right next to mine.'

Nic let out a huge belch. 'I'd appreciate that. Hope the food is as good as the pay.'

'It's not but it's edible. Better than the shit you've been eating.'

Nic harrumphed, hitching up his collar. 'Some of it was damn fine. You're just jealous because you're restricted in who you fraternise with.'

'Could be. We only get approved hookers once a month. At least they're clean and free.'

Nic thought about that. Approved meant security and drug screened. Not many hookers he knew would subject themselves to those processes unless it was worth it. He wondering how rich Hedonia City really was. The docking fees for the shuttles would add up. There was at least ten of them a week, not including the support craft with supplies. Legit sex and drugs were taxed and he guessed all the imported food was too. Then there were the lease fees. No one could own any part of the city, it belonged to the city council corporation.

After a good breakfast next morning, Nic dressed in his new uniform, feeling a sense of pride that had been absent from his life for quite a while. With a smile on his face, he reported for his first day at work. For the most part, he observed, listening to 'fuckface' all day until he yawned.

The routine continued day after day. His nights were plagued with flashbacks of his time with the transmuter, memories and dreams merged together. The alien couldn't

11

get enough of him. Give me more, it would demand. You must get me more. He'd start over, feeling exhausted on waking.

After two weeks on the job, Nic was convinced it was all a sham. No one really had the specs down. They cleaned ventilations shafts, undid panels, inspected the alien contents and sealed them up again. Either they didn't trust him or something weird was going on.

At the Zephyr, Nic raised the question with Johann. The engineer shook his head. 'I've been here three years. I've seen no specs, no engine designs, no documented schematics of the alien technology. There's been one or two overhauls of the turbines in my time and the occasional aoleus gas measurement.'

'You don't find that curious? Odd even?'

'I get paid. I keep my mouth shut. The less I know the better. Why are you so interested?'

Nic shrugged. 'Just am. Logical isn't it?'

Johann cast him a strange look. 'Maybe.'

'What about the sinking sections of the city. Have you worked on those ever in the last three years?'

Johann swallowed another mouthful and shook his head. 'Most crews get a rotation to different parts of the undercity. I can't say I've known of any who have worked there. There are eleven crews. I don't do the rosters.' He shrugged and took another long drink.

Nic took another drink himself, letting their conversation settle in his mind. His gaze lingered on the dance floor, remembering how it felt to be in a narc haze with women panting to get into his trousers, throwing money at him to pleasure them. Had male to female relationships always been one of commerce? At least he had left the women satisfied, if somewhat poorer. He

12

wondered now if that job had more meaning than the current one.

Then there were the disappearance and the deaths. Another engineer had mysteriously disappeared in the past week. Rumour had it that he was dead. Nic had not met him and had no real idea how he had died or if he had. Everyone was tight-lipped, saying it was for the official investigation to reveal. There had been rumours that there was no body, so how did they know he died? Now when he thought about the absence of a real knowledge base about the alien technology that kept Hedonia floating, he wondered if there was a connection. Had these engineers found out too much? Had they disobeyed the rules, broke silence? What silence? There was nothing to tell. Nic shrugged, not really caring if people saw that he was thinking and not paying attention to his surroundings.

That night he found it hard to sleep. Tossing and turning didn't help, didn't relieve the tension. His mind had a problem to solve and in his dream state, he thought he had worked out how the turbines worked. Even his transmuter lover was sated. When he woke the next morning it was there, but just out of reach.

The next day he was with a work crew assigned to one of the gantries that he had seen on his first day. The wind was up but the gantry provided shelter as well as a way into one of the access chutes on a secondary gas intake valve. Nic was meant to watch and learn, still not trusted to use his brain or skill or hands for that matter. His hair ruffled in the wind, making him wish he'd cut it when he had the chance the day before. He tried to stay focussed but his gaze kept straying to one of the arched doorways further along the walkway. An unsecured door open and shut as he looked on. He had the urge to investigate, stronger and stronger. A sharp headache made him gasp.

While the others were engaged in securing their lines and readying their cleaning equipment, Nic stole up the walkway toward it, the pain in his head waning with each step he took. He put his hand on the door, feeling the greasy layer of fungi and pushed the door wide open. It was dark on the inside.

'Hello? Anyone there?' he called out.

No one replied or objected to his being there. Casting a glance back at the work crew, he saw that they hadn't noticed his absence. He took a step and placed himself inside the threshold, shutting the door behind him. A dull green light grew steadily brighter as he leaned his back against the door. Nic's heart thumped. He heard the door click and quickly turned to open it. The lock had engaged sealing the door tight. He didn't panic as the crew would come looking for him.

The room grew steadily brighter and he edged around to look at his surroundings. A long corridor stretched out in front of him. In the distance shadows moved and leapt as light beamed in through tall, thin windows. A low hum vibrated along the floor planking and he thought he heard the sounds of voices and heavy objects being dragged along metal floors. He took a few steps along the corridor, the light brightening with each step.

He tried to work out which section he was in. The sealed one? Something about a university research project or was it the unsafe areas sealed by the city? The construction in this section looked sound to him. All that was absent was the alien scrollwork and wall carvings. This walls were made of metal, gold tinged metal. Looking up he saw the distant ceiling appeared draped in growths, more like cobwebs than anything else could name.

The voices grew more distinct and Nic slowed his pace, hoping to mask the sound of his footsteps. Then so suddenly, he almost missed it, a wide archway appeared to his left. He was standing in the middle of it before he was aware of it. The light was dimmer there, lit by small telltale winking lights on banks of machinery. Nic sucked in a breath and let it out slowly. There was nothing for it. He'd come this far so he stepped into the room. He forgot to breathe at first. There was no one in the room, just machinery, computers banks by the looks of them, humming away. With a raised eyebrow, he turned full circle, seeing power cables snaking along the floor and out through a specially cut hole in the wall. Looked modern to him. Not the ancient alien tech. He turned back to the hallway and continued on.

As he walked the voices alternated from becoming clear and distinct, to muffled. He thought there could be three people ahead. The next opening did not take him by surprise. Light speared out through the open doorway and a manshape moved into the farther dimness ahead of him before passing out of view.

Hard against the wall, Nic stood still and then quickly stuck his head around to take in the scene. He pulled back quickly, heart pounding. There were at least five people in there, all checking the monitors of strange looking containers, which looked like ancient sarcophagi, with ornate designs carved into them.

He tried for one more look, raking his gaze quickly and carefully over the room. Then deciding he'd seen enough he tensed to bolt along the corridor only to be brought up short by a man holding a weapon and blocking his exit. The nozzle of the gun pointed at Nic's chest. Judging by the uniform and the professional looking stance, the guy was military. The guy jerked the business end of his gun twice in the direction of the room. Shocked gasps echoed around them as they entered. Turning his gaze to the bank of sarcophagi, Nic blanched and took a step back, nearly stumbling.

'Found him spying on you from the corridor,' said the guy with the gun.

A woman stepped forward, checking him over, looking him up and down. 'A wayward engineer? A new one I expect. The other ones know better than to stick their nose in where they are not wanted.'

'Look I'm sorry for disturbing you. I'll just go.'

'Not so fast.' The nozzle of the gun pointed directly at him. She read his nametag, then took out her personal assistant and scrolled the screen, eyes tracking the text. 'Yes, good stats here. He'd make a suitable engineer.' Her dark eyes appraised him. She turned away and went to the far sarcophagus. Leaning over it, she checked some readouts, which looked like modern additions to the alien tech. 'The old one is passing, may not last the day.'

She walked back toward him, finger tapping on her chin, brows cinched in thought.

'The new recruit didn't cope...we are running out of time.'

The nozzle of the gun rose higher. 'You wanna use him?'

'He's got good stats. He wants to be an engineer. We'll have to risk it and make him a real one.' She turned to Nic. 'Strip.'

'Can you tell me what is going on? What are those things?'

'Shut up and get your gear off.' Her eyes were hard. She meant business.

A quick scan of the military bloke's expression convinced him his choices were non-existent. Nic undid his uniform, sliding it off his shoulders and dropping it to the floor. The woman's eyebrow lifted as her gaze went over his body. 'A bit of a waste, maybe.'

A man who had been monitoring the other sarcophagi came forward, jerked Nic's hands behind his back and tied them. Around Nic's neck, the man attached a tether. Nic inhaled sharply as the crackle of power constricted his breathing, bent him over double in pain. Now it was time to get scared.

They walked him closer to the sarcophagi. A couple had old shrivelled beings in them. Lynex he guessed. So much for there not been much known about them. They had had live specimens right in the city all the time. He supposed the city council didn't want to lessen the mystery of the floating city. It might damage their revenues. The other three held humans, all males. Missing engineers perhaps.

'Get him to the prep table,' ordered the woman.

A shove from behind made Nic stumble. 'No wait. I won't tell anyone. You don't need to do this. I'm new here.'

'Shut up. Not interested.'

'Look I only wanted to know how the tech worked. Wanted to understand.'

He was pushed down on a long table, his neck tether immobilising him when the woman engaged the control. 'Well Mr Da Silva, you are going to find out all you wanted to know and more. If the incorporation goes well, you'll enjoy a nice long life.'

They inserted canulas into the veins of his arms and legs, shoved choking feeding tubes down his throat, poked a catheter into his penis and brought over a surgical tray and prepped him for surgery. Nic couldn't even scream as they cut into his skin. The med tech did the cutting.

'Sorry for the discomfort but you won't need to shit no more. This nice little stoma will connect you nicely to the equipment. Once you're inserted, we'll take the rest of your intestines out. They tend to rot after a few years. Took us a while to work that out.'

Nic lost consciousness then. From fear, pain or drugs he did not know. When he came to he was deep in the unit. He felt a strange presence next to him, inside him. It cocooned him, stroked him, joined with him as relaxants pulsed through his blood stream. Once the connection was complete, white pain, searing consciousness-killing agony, enveloped him.

Too stunned to think of screaming, he blinked through the worst of it and then there was knowledge. When he saw it, saw the extent of it, he laughed in his mind. It was all there, all the answers to the puzzling mystery of the floating city. The schematics, the maps of circuits, the fault logs, the long history of Hedonia stretching out inside of him. Now he knew what kept the city floating, he knew all the secrets, he could even tap into those new machines, the puny things the interlopers had tried to interface with the Lynex technology. His senses reached out, he breathed with the city, breathed with the minds connected to its apparatus.

Abruptly, his body jerked and twitched. Something was wrong. He could sense/hear alarms. Then a new, but familiar presence appeared. It! The transmuter. Big and live and victorious. Not it, an image, an avatar. Damn that was why his head ached. It had left a probe there in his head, filtering information, urging him on. Its program began to suck, to process all the new found knowledge, encode it and then transmit it. Nic detected it flowing, the facts, the equations, the schematics leaking away, unable to fight the brain drain.

Somewhere within the vast information network of the city, a defensive program initiated. The transmuter's program shrieked as her avatar erupted into blue hot flame, winking out silently as the probe was destroyed. Nic felt satisfaction. He hope it hurt it, but knew it was only a program not the transmuter inside his head.

Nic wondered if they had killed it in time. He thought so. The knowledge contained within the mind of the city was extensive. It would take him many lifetimes to understand it all, to learn it all. He was ready. Now he knew what it meant to be an engineer in the floating city.

Author Note

This story was inspired by a trip to Venice. A beautiful place in elegant decline and I thought what if this was a floating city in orbit around a planet. I liked the mystery of lost races, too, those that leave hints of their passing but you can never really know what they were like, what they thought about and how they lived.

Green, Green Grass of Homeworld

The hiss of steam teased Vo-nam D'abela's sensitive ears as hypodermic needles retracted from veins in arms, legs and tail. Antiseptic stung the pinprick wounds as he flexed his limbs. As stasis induced fugue sloughed off, his heart rate quickened and breaths deepened. He had arrived.

A harsh stench washed over him as he opened his eyes. The refuse of year's assisted life-support flushed away, leaving its fetid aftermath lingering on his tongue. When his eyesight cleared, he saw that his wife's stasis unit was vacant and sanitised, ready for the next occupant. He frowned at Li-pen's absence.

Perhaps Li-pen had been revived before him and had left on some errand for surely she had not gone to see Earth without him. She had not wanted to come with him on this trip, despite her being part human like him. The money, the time were only some of the excuses she used to delay them taking this trip. The fact that they had no offspring, and hence no ties to Dianur, had been the deciding factor. But Vo-nam had waited his whole life to come to the homeworld and to see Earth in its majesty, its blueness radiant in the black firmament of space. For so long he had pictured it in his mind's eye, dreamt it after staring at images of the planet for hours and hours. Anxiety about Li-pen's absence lessened when he thought she was probably in the transition lounge, wondering why it was taking him so long to wake up.

The monitor chimed, telling him that his body was now in normal state. With a certain amount of regret, he saw while dressing that his soft, downy coat had faded to a dun colour. He wondered what the Earth's atmosphere would do to it. Would his pelt glow golden under Sol's rays, like great grandfather Luis D'abela had said it would? Would it ever regain the sheen years of careful grooming and doenut oil had enlivened? A glowing pelt was a matter of pride for a Di-Nuk, a Nuk of mixed species like him. There was something about those human genes that brought out the best in the Nuk physique. He was taller, more muscular and out-performed pure Nuk academically. Pity that his kin did not value the benefits of his mixed heritage or recognise the injection of superior human DNA into their gene pool. Vo-nam growled as he tried to bury the memories, the shame. No recognition from his extended family, no jobs, no housing and no social services.

Not that there was any official discrimination of Di-Nuk. No, thought Vo-nam, the unofficial was severe enough. It was so bad that Vo-nam had been raised under the Post-Colonial Dependents scheme, a small fund to look after what the Earth settlers and their technological intervention had left behind. Li-pen had never qualified for the scheme, except as his dependent. With the final proceeds of his trust fund, they could finally connect with their human heritage. Soon he would touch the soil of the homeworld, a place where he really belonged.

The door shushed open as he exited the life-support suite. Li-pen was not in the lounge as he had thought. Although he would never tell her so, he was annoyed that she had not waited for him. He could not help the feelings that swelled inside of him. The first view of the homeworld was a moment for sharing. He found it hard to go against that cultural imperative—not to speak his mind—ever.

Pity Li-pen was not impeded by it. To his dismay, she never failed to speak her mind to him.

He followed the corridor that led to the observation deck. His thumping heartbeat spurring him to walk faster. Staff and passengers intermingled, a mixture of Nuk, humans and the glossy skinned Lumko. Vo-nam tried not to stare. They had been advised at boarding that they would be taking on Lumko refugees at Killen station, but still the sight of one so alien drew his curiosity. Lumko had near translucent skin, so that the shadows of their blood vessels and organs were visible. They could see but their eyes were under the skin at the side of their heads, like a kind of mutated fish that he had seen in one of the Earth children's books. He had heard that the Lumko could speak with each other through smells, grunts and gestures. That they walked around naked was also difficult to ignore. Vo-nam caught himself tugging the waistline of his kilt higher. Looking down, he adjusted the sash crossing his chest so that it disguised his central breast. His tail brushed the ground behind him, sweeping the floor slowly. Luckily, the Lumko wore tech translators so that non-Lumko could understand them, not that Vo-nam would dare to attempt to converse with one.

As he traversed the corridor, he tried to keep his excitement and awe in check, angling his head down and walking straight and true like a human, rather than when he was in Dianur and had had to imitate the pure bloods by walking slightly sideways and with a loping gait and bouncing tail. He found he was concentrating so hard on maintaining his walk that he missed the access port to the observation deck and had to backtrack, dodging a steward weaving through the crowds with a tray of beverages. The steward then disappeared into a private function room further along the corridor. Vo-nam did his best not to peer through the door when it swung open. Voices spilled out and he caught glimpses of humans and others before the door slid shut.

When he entered the observation deck, he saw family groups, some peering and pointing down to the blue planet. A few singletons stood by, gazing at the view. Most were human but there were one or two other Di-Nuks. The sight of Earth through the viewing pane, drew all of Vo-nam's attention. He just stood and gaped as he entered and completely forgot about the people around him and finding Li-pen. It was not until there were protests behind him did he realise that he had blocked the doorway, thereby preventing other newly-awakened travellers from entering and seeing the blue planet in all its glory. Bowing his head and muttering apologies like a cowering Di-Nuk, he backed away. Realising his lapse, he straightened up and strode purposefully to the viewing deck. There was no need to observe the Dianuran social norms now that he was on Earth. He did not need to apologise for who he was, or feel the need to make abeyances to his superiors. On Earth all were equal.

Li-pen touched his arm gently, startling him. He did not know how long he had been there; it could have been hours or only minutes such was his absorption. Her grin showed her fine pointed teeth, which allowed her to pass for a Nuk most of the time. As he looked at her again after their long sleep, he admired Li-pen's prettiness and intelligence. Her body shape was very Nuk and her pelt was slightly mauve in colour. Under the ship's lights, it had taken on a silver sheen. Usually, she let her coat grow shaggy, a quaint habit, that let her blend in more with the pure bloods. Vo-nam liked to appear well groomed even though that set him apart. Great grandfather Luis had instilled the need for grooming into him and told him many a time that he was special to have human DNA. *Lucky to have it you are. Only the special ones could take it you know. It will benefit you one day, lad, it will. Mark my words, mark them well.* With a quick glance out the window, he grinned. It would be his time soon.

'I did not see you, Li. I was so taken by the view of the homeworld. Forgive me, I did not ignore you on purpose.'

Li smiled again, her gaze flicking to the doorway and beyond before returning to him.

'I understand, Vo,' patting his arm. 'You have waited long for this. I should tell you though, and I'm not sure how this will affect you...I mean us...but the DNA profiles for visa classes has changed since we boarded.'

Vo-nam shrugged and grunted. 'I am part human that is enough to let me get a visa. I cannot see how they can change that fundamental right.'

Li frowned. 'Vo...they can deny you a visa or restrict the class of visa depending on their rules. They make the rules and can change them. I'm not saying it will affect us, only that I heard talk and wanted to warn you in case...'

Vo-nam found his mood had soured. 'We should perhaps check which shuttle we are on and secure our luggage.'

Li slid her hand down his forearm. 'Yes, Vo. Let's do that. Immigration and customs are planet side so we'll find out then.'

***

The entry hall at the London Customs Hall was full of milling people, voices churning and the occasional holler. Vo stood opposite the customs official, with his tail twitching and his hackles rising.

'What do you mean that I can only get a short stay tourist visa? I was advised not to apply for my visa before I left so that it would have more time on it. Now you are saying I can only enter if I agree to return in four weeks? That means I would have to leave on the ship I have just arrived on, which departs in two weeks or otherwise I'd be in breach.'

Li stood beyond the barrier, her visa processed and watched him as he listened with growing horror the effect of the DNA matrix assessment had on his right to land on the homeworld. The official had already explained things to him but Vo-nam couldn't believe it. His outrage drove all common sense from his mind. Anger was ripping through his blood. Only the quiet words from Li-pen penetrated long enough for him to calm down. He felt the need to reach out and squeeze with his clawed hands. He had waited so long for this moment. He had held the rage in check. All those times he had been excluded in the past. All those times where he was not welcomed and he could not show the hurt and the pain because he was Di-Nuk and to do so would betray his human heritage and would bring disrespect to all Di-Nuk and further shame. He remembered the whispered phrases from his childhood days. *Those hybrids are unstable. The human DNA makes them violent. Crazy even.* He remembered the shunning, the avoidance as if it was yesterday.

'I am sorry, Mr D'abela. The Colonial Statutes for mixed race species were amended six months ago and enacted three months ago, which means they are in force now. Your visa could not be processed at your point of origin because of the pending changes and you were advised to apply at the border accordingly. You can have a nice visit here for a couple of weeks. The tourist areas will provide ample opportunity to sample contemporary Earth life.'

'Sample?' Vo-nam sucked in a breath fighting for calm. 'But I want to live it, experience it. My wife's visa was processed without these problems. Why?'

The official turned to glance at Li-pen, his microbe shields glistening wetly in his nostrils. He faced Vo-nam again. 'I am afraid that due to privacy concerns I cannot discuss your wife's status. You will have to apply to her for an explanation, although she is under no obligation to do so and her rights are protected under Earth law. However, you will deduce that there is some difference in the human DNA between you.'

Li-pen drew closer and touched his arm, stroking the down near his wrist. 'Vo, accept the visa so we can get to our hotel. We can try to sort things out later. We will lodge another application at the local office. Please, I am very tired now.'

Turning, Li-pen nodded to the official, which was an action too subservient for Vo-nam's peace of mind. The official slid the visa card into Vo-nam's passport and passed it across the counter before calling out. 'Next.'

Vo-nam lowered his head, fighting for a dignity he felt had been stripped away. The feeling was more than disappointment but he could not articulate it to himself. With a glance at Li-pen's eager gaze as she took in the crowd and urged him into the transit queue, he felt he could not even begin to tell her either.

***

The transit to their Bath hotel was a blur. The visa issue loomed large in Vo-nam's mind and it soured the first scents of Earth's air. The green fields that surrounded Bath were a smear of treeless countryside that barely registered. The district's atmospheric shield shimmered in the sunlight. The Austen complex gleamed with freshly

27

polished Georgian stone or so Li explained to him, reading from her guide book. There were only a few places on Earth that Vo-nam's restricted visa allowed him to go and the tourist area of Wiltshire was the most appealing and economical of them.

The relic of London city and its underground hotels held no appeal to someone from Nuk heritage. The trees and open skies were important and in the pre-flight education program, he had been warned that Nuk did not fare well in the dark, damp underground places. Stories of psychosis abounded and of the accidental execution of Nuks, who had lost control and stormed through the corridors. Vo-nam considered himself mostly human, but could not deny that there was a deep, inexplicable fear of being closed in and being held underground. Li often lectured him on his tendency to ignore that he had an equal Nuk DNA makeup. There were also the cultural imperatives from living on Dianur that could override any inherited human traits.

Li-pen drew her gaze from the guide book when the vehicle stopped. 'Lo, cheer up, Vo. We will do some interesting things while we are here. You make too much of being part human you know.'

Vo could only stare at her and nod dumbly. Soon after, the bellbot delivered them and their luggage to a room on the top floor. Vo went to the windows and saw the views reaching out across lush green hills with puffed white sheep standing idle. While he stood there, Li-pen set about unpacking and arranging their things, talking to Vo-nam all the while and explaining where and why she was putting things. Vo-nam let her voice soothe him. Soon it would be time to eat.

Vo-nam gazed out of the window until sunset. When it was too dark to see he picked up the guide book and flipped through the pages idly. As the pages whisked by he wondered if it would tell him where he could get fresh killed game. Great grandfather Luis had told him that there was plenty of food on Earth and the people often ate fresh killed deer, or bears, or birds. Thinking about the landscape though, he could not think where the game would live. There were no trees, only pastures. Perhaps it was the sheep that were now hunted for food.

After breakfast the next morning, the hotel liaison recommended a day tour of the Bath region. Li-pen said yes before Vo-nam could speak.

'I thought we should go to the immigration office and see about changing my visa status,' he whispered urgently in her ear.

'There's no hurry,' she whispered back, while bowing her head to the hotel liaison. 'Come on, I want to play tourist today. Think of me for a change.'

She patted him on the arm and then scratched him under the chin. Vo-nam lowered his head and nodded. He would be patient.

The remains of the Roman baths were extremely ancient. The water still trickled up through the spring but the walls and the Roman statues were now replicas of the original remains. Vo-nam found it quite boring, despite Li-pen's obvious enthusiasm. She asked to tour guide to explain.

'A very good question,' the tour guide replied. Li-pen grinned and nodded to Vo-nam. 'By removing the originals and replacing them with the replicas we can best preserve the heritage of the area and still provide the look and feel of the times.'

With a smile, Li-pen followed the guide onto the bus, leaving Vo-nam to make his own way. As they drove around, Vo-nam could see a few people dressed in period clothing. Vo-nam thought that was strange, but Li-pen read from the guidebook, which stated that the re-enactment was to help visitors to picture Earth's past, the days when there was tranquillity and little or no technology.

As they drove along a road, past featureless pastures, Vo-nam thought that Dianur had such political sentiments. That was why the humans were ousted around one hundred Earth years previously. Nuk were rural. They lived close to nature, in clans. While some of the clans found human technology seductive, others found it pervasive and subversive. In school, Vo-nam had studied the re-establishment of home rule and the effects it had. It mattered not to him on an emotional level that the resentment of his mixed heritage was based on the political shenanigans of the time. Home rule did lead to a resurgence of historical backward looking and glorification of the past. Many clans purged themselves of human technology and reverted to pre-colonial methods of food production and manufacturing. In some cases the resentment went deep. So much so that his parents had been killed during a purge and he had been brought up in the human protectorate by his uncle.

Ah, Uncle Vin, thought Vo-nam, feeling his eye lids grow heavy as the bus ride lulled his senses. Long dead now was Uncle Vin but he remembered his voice. *Should have taken us all back to Earth. What's the point of maintaining the protectorate? Costs them loads and is so unwieldy. Must be some other reason, something they are not saying.* Vin often repeated this opinion after he had made his way home from one too many Gin and Tonics in the protectorate bar. After his uncle's death, Vo had to integrate into Nuk society as part of his transition program.

Once again at the hotel, Vo-nam stared out the window, looking across the city to the fields beyond. He felt himself frowning again and went to brush his pelt. He was not happy with the colour of his coat. It was dull grey in the Earth light and thinking about Uncle Vin reminded him that he could not imbibe alcohol at all. It had nearly killed him the only time he had tried. All pure Nuk could not metabolise alcohol. It was a sore point with him. Something that made him feel less human instead of more.

Again the next day, Li-pen insisted that they play tourist. Vo-nam held his peace. The tour guide stopped the bus in Wells so that they could view the cathedral, now preserved under a transparent dome. Clockwork knights came in and out of compartments located in the side of the building. Vo-nam yawned while drinking coffee and eating cucumber sandwiches.

'These are tasteless. Why do we not have a hamburger like him over there?' Vo pointed to another patron, who bit down on the meat and juices dripped down his clean shaven chin.

Li-pen nudged his arm. 'Shush now. This is the most traditional of meals, you know. Royalty used to eat it every day. Come on, eat up. The bus will leave soon.'

By the time they were returned to their hotel, Vo-nam's stomach was rumbling. As he had not seen fresh game on the hotel menu the previous night, he had decided that they should venture out on their own and prowl the streets of Bath for a suitable restaurant.

He thought it was odd that the concierge quizzed them about where they were going and how long they were going to be away. He asked for their visa tag numbers so that he could contact them in case of an emergency. Vo-nam was ready to make a curt response but Li-pen was there bowing her head and shuffling them out the door subserviently. Vo worried about Li's behaviour. Normally she would stand up for herself. Mentally shrugging, he realised that travelling to new places put a strain on people. His reactions were not normal for him so he supposed Li was allowed to be affected in some way too.

The night air was so moist that Vo-nam felt his spirits lift. His annoyance and Li-pen's insistence on a subservient attitude slid away. This was the homeworld that his great grandfather has spoken about, kindling Vo-nam's own desire to know his human heritage.

Again, the streets were rather bare of people. Tourists like themselves appeared to be the only ones around. Some of the tourists were human. They travelled in groups and often whispered when they neared any Di-Nuk.

'Surely they know we are part human and have native rights to visit and live on Earth,' Vo-nam whispered to his wife. Well except for me, as I have a tourist visa, he thought sourly.

'Lo, don't let it up set you, Vo. Not everyone is as well-educated as you. And perhaps they don't see many Di-Nuks where they come from.'

Outside one restaurant, Li-pen stopped him from entering. 'Not that one. Let's find somewhere else,' she suggested, tugging on his arm, her tail agitated. He resisted and went to step through the door. He was keen to try the restaurant because all the patrons appeared to be human.

Li-pen started to walk away and he was left holding the doorknob. He dropped his hand and followed after her. She had the credit cards after all.

'Why did you do that?' he asked as he trailed his wife down the street.

'Because I want a nice quiet dinner without you getting paranoid about humans and their reactions to us.

You expect too much from them just like you do pure bloods at home.'

'But...but...'

Li-pen walked faster and Vo had to hurry to keep up with her. The restaurants seemed to peter out after two intersections and Li-pen slowed down. There was an alleyway leading to a courtyard and another street beyond. Vo-nam thought he saw people walking there and headed off in that direction. Li-pen followed without complaint.

Vo-nam stood stock still and saw a number of rectangular vehicles with small windows cut into them. A quick glance and he could tell most of them were roboservers. However, in one of them a Di-Nuk handed out food to customers. Spices, sweet sauces and an array of food smells mingled in the courtyard. Immediately, Vo was drawn the cart manned by the Di-Nuk. As he neared, the tantalising scent of seared meat teased his nostrils. Beside him, Li-pen growled low in her throat, unable to deny her reaction to the closeness of the food. The Di-Nuk's eyes widened when he saw them.

'Not often we see Di-Nuks here in the back street. What can I get you?' His accent was rather strange. He spoke like his vowels had been flattened and his consonants sharpened. Vo-nam was not certain but he sensed that the food vendor was nervous.

Glancing at the price list, which was more than half what the hotel charged, Vo-nam licked his fangs with a wet tongue. 'Meat for both of us. Rare if possible,' he requested in his best Earth tongue.

'Sure. Coming right up.' The vendor sliced off thick slaps of meat from a joint he had grilling and placed it between two large pieces of bread. 'You want sauce?'

Looking at the vender sideways, Vo asked him in Nuk. 'Do you have any Dinuda?'

The vendor frowned so Vo-nam spoke in the Earth tongue again.

The Di-Nuk nodded. 'No, what about sweet chilli? It's good.'

'Thank you, yes.' Vo-nam glanced at his wife. Did that mean this Di-Nuk had never tasted Dinuda sauce? he thought. Ignoring his look, Li-pen paid for the food, and they stood to the side to eat it. Li-pen's gaze tracked the movements of the vendor as he served other customers. There was nowhere to sit and as Li-pen seemed as curious as he was to learn more of the strange speaking Di-Nuk, they loitered nearby, waiting for an opportunity to engage him in conversation again.

'So do you live around here?' Li-pen asked, when she caught the vendor's eye.

The vendor began cleaning the bench inside his window. 'Not far from here.'

'So you live in the tourist zone?' Vo asked, excited by the prospect.

'No, not really. No.'

'So you have a work visa?' Vo asked.

The vendor's eyes arrowed around the courtyard and he began packing things away. 'I have a visa but technically I'm not meant to sell produce here in the tourist zone. I don't usually but I heard there was a ship in and I thought I might attract some of the tourist crowd.'

'So you are Di-Nuk like us but you speak differently. Why is that?'

The vendor looked uncomfortable. He leant out of the window saw there was no other customers and undid the lever that held the window shutter up. 'Sorry. I've got to head off now. Nice meeting you.'

Vo-nam stepped forward and held the shutter open. 'Please talk to us. We really want to know and we won't tell anyone else if it bothers you.'

'I can't say, truly. It's difficult.'

Li-pen swallowed the last of her meat and bread. 'You were brought up on Earth, weren't you? That is why you speak like that, why you can't speak Nuk well at all.'

Vo-nam gaped at his wife and the vendor. 'Is that true? How could that be? I thought none of the hybrids were brought to Earth.'

The food vendor's hand was on the shutter ready to jerk in down. 'I said I can't talk about it.'

'So it is true? Will you be here tomorrow? Can we talk to you again?' Vo-Nam asked politely, bowing his head to show humility. His tail lowered and swept the ground from side to side with slow grace.

'Sure. I'll be here around sunset.'

Vo-nam let his hand drop and the shutter closed with a clang. Soon after the vehicle powered up and lumbered out of the courtyard.

Vo walked with Li-pen to their hotel in the Austen complex. A group of people in Regency dress walked past them, laughing and chatting gaily. Vo frowned, finding he did not like the historic trappings of Bath. He wanted to see the real homeworld as it was now.

That night while he slept he thought up a plan. No more guided tours. He would sneak out and take a look at what they hide from the tourists. It was easy to exit the hotel before dawn without being noticed. There were nothing but cleaning bots and a sleepy receptionist in the foyer.

Vo-nam had left his wife asleep, hoping to be back before she woke up. It appeared she was able to survive on tea and toast. He found he needed much more meat than was on offer and wanted to make sure he got something more substantial to eat. Yet the hotel charged a lot of money for any kind of meat. It was either scarce or the owners were vegetarians and were eager to push their creed onto others.

The sun was not quite up and the street lights were still shining when he made it out onto the road. No people were about as far as he could see. He chose a street at random and walked down it. As the sky grew brighter, he thought that the edge of town might appeal. Perhaps he would find some trees, some wildlife (food) or least some real people going about their early morning business.

The empty streets and houses made him edgy. He supposed there were people in the houses and apartments but he was not convinced. Yet why would they be uninhabited? The air felt clean, the town was pleasant in an odd, historical kind of way. Why did he get the sense that he was alone? The scents too were stale, like people had passed this way once, long ago and never returned.

At the edge of town, a park called Hampton Down segued into pasture. There were a few sheep there, standing still on a slope. A small pond had ducks floating on it, an occasional quack audible. There was even a rabbit dashing in and out of a burrow, its cotton tail dancing tantalisingly. Soft undulating hills further on had sheep on them too.

Vo-nam found the scene quite pleasing until he heard voices. Suddenly he felt guilty, realising that perhaps he was where he should not be. Looking around for a place to hide, he found a stone monument and placed himself behind it. The monument commemorated something called Bath Golf Course, 1880 -2050. His pelt matched the colour of the stone so he felt sure he blended in. While he watched, two humans came into view, males he thought they were, and each was holding an end of a sheep. Vo tried hear what they were saying but they were talking so fast, he found it hard to catch the words.

They positioned the sheep, opened the side of it up and tinkered with its insides before shutting what looked like a panel. Then one man went to the head and tilted it back as if it was connected by hinge. 'Ahhh, here it is,' the workman said in a slow, drawling way. 'Short circuit.' The other man's reply was muffled as he was bent over wiping the hooves of the sheep with a dusting cloth. Then the dialogue between them became incomprehensible again. They spoke in some kind of rhyme and half sentences. Some words he could catch but the meaning was lost on him. Closing up the sheep, the men walked away, still bantering with each other and laughing occasionally. Vo-nam ducked down to avoid being seen as the workman walked away. As the sound of the conversation faded, Vo-nam put his head around the monument and peeked out.

The sheep bleated once and then moved slightly, giving the impression of life. Vo-nam felt suddenly ill. Next, he found himself gasping for breath, heart palpitating painfully. What did that mean? It couldn't be a live animal. His mind was working furiously, re-jigging all of his impressions and thoughts of Earth with those of his earlier expectations and beliefs. They did not marry up well at all. If the sheep were fake, what else? After the workmen disappeared from view, he crept over to the pasture and touched it. Going down on all fours, he sniffed it and then tasted it. Fake. It was some kind of resin, not real grass.

Still disbelieving he then padded up to the pond. The ducks did not react to his presence. He squatted down, watched them, listened for the quacks. There! The sound but no beaks moved. Sniffing, he found no scents. The pond smelt too fresh and chemical. The rabbit moved again, sprinting from its burrow. Vo-nam growled at it. The rabbit didn't even flinch. He watched it further and saw that it too, was following some predetermined routine.

This was beyond belief. He could understand the replica monuments and even the re-enactments with menus and period dress—but the animals and the vegetation? What had happened to the homeworld his great grandfather Luis had told him about and the books which backed up those tales?

He found his head swimming. Facts and fiction were stitched together like some sick tapestry. It was hard to take in. His homeworld was a fake. A replica. A façade. Lo, a tourist trap. Vo-nam sprawled in the grass, struggling to control his feelings, to compartmentalise his pain, his anger, his disappointment. The sun was well up by the time he decided to head back to the hotel.

Li-Pen was eating toast and jam when he entered the room. She looked up as he slammed the door behind him. 'Lo, good morning, husband. I have ordered eggs for you. It was the best I could do on our budget. Where have you been?'

He nodded. 'Out,' he replied and sat down to stare at his plate. He did not know how to tell her how he felt about what he had seen. He did not know if she would understand. He had dragged her here to this fake homeworld. It was his fault, his responsibility.

'Are you going to eat that? If not, I am still hungry.' Li-Pen said, fork poised to spear a mound of scrambled egg.

Coming out of his reverie, he growled low in his throat, which translated to 'my food, back off.'

Li-Pen laughed and reclined back on the bed. 'Lo, that is more like it. So tell me what did you see or do that upset your appetite?'

He tried to explain to Li-Pen what he saw. She nodded and scrunched up her nose, a Nuk characteristic for puzzlement. 'So the sheep are fake? It is a tourist zone so I suppose none of it would be real.'

'What about the grass? It is fake too. Why would anyone fake vegetation unless it is all gone.'

Li-pen got up and began to brush her coat with vigorous, sharp strokes. 'You are making a big deal out of nothing. I agree it is a puzzle but ...not...a conspiracy.' She continued her grooming and after a few minutes asked brightly, 'So what should we do today?' She looked in the mirror as she ruffled her coat with her fingers to make a random pattern.

'The immigration office opens at eight,' he replied, grinning.

She turned to look at him and shook her head. 'Not today, Vo. I cannot face arguing with bureaucracy. Maybe tomorrow. Mmmm?' She frowned and bared her teeth.

Vo-nam nodded. There was no point in arguing with her. He knew that look. At that moment too, he wondered if he really wanted to stay, now that he knew. But what choice did he have? He did not belong on Dianur. He was not one of them.

So they readied themselves for more tourist adventures, with Li-Pen at least agreeing to see the Earth-raised Di-Nuk at sunset. After returning from viewing a dome with standing stones in it and the facade of Salisbury Cathedral, they snuck out of the hotel again, avoiding the questions from the concierge.

There were many people around the vending vans when they arrived. Vo-nam hung back waiting for the last of the customers to slip into the growing shadows. A few of the other vendors closed up shop and trundled out of the courtyard on noisy motors. Most of the customers were

39

human tourists, getting a thrill from buying real meat at affordable prices. From overhearing the various conversations, these humans were from off world and enjoying visiting the homeworld too. Vo did his best not to envy their humanness.

The Di-Nuk lowered the shutter. Vo-Nam's ears pricked up. Was he leaving? But then he heard the whispered call from behind the van. Li-Pen and Vo-nam headed around the back of the vehicle to see him. The Di-Nuk was short and his tail was pushed into his human clothes. Through his open shirt, Vo could see several surgical scars.

'What is your name?' Vo asked, completely mesmerised by what he was seeing. The Di-Nuk's gait was slightly off and his mannerisms were almost completely human. The Di-Nuk smiled like a human, his teeth square. Were they filed? thought Vo-nam.

'Round here they call me Petey.'

'You have a human name?' Li-Pen asked. 'What about your clan?'

Petey shrugged, using the human gesture. 'Don't know who my clan are. Don't know who my kin are. I'm an orphan.'

Vo-nam tried not to think of the possibilities that were denied him because he had a living uncle and had stayed on Dianur. He had been orphaned and could have been brought up on Earth like this Di-Nuk.

'So tell us then. What do robot sheep mean?' Vo-Nam asked, surprised he had taken on his wife's outspoken characteristics. Why had he not beaten around the forest to scare out the game, as the saying went on Dianur.

'You saw?' The Di-Nuk nodded and scratched his chin. Another human gesture. It made Vo's stomach turn and he shook himself, realising that this is what pure Nuk must feel when they looked at him. A parody of a Nuk. It was not a happy realisation. 'It's all fake.'

Li-Pen had been eying Petey with curiosity. 'Where do you live, Petey?'

Petey looked around assuring himself that they were alone. 'I live in the enclaves near here. Technically, I don't have a license to sell food in the zone but competition is tough for the likes of me.'

'What do you mean? Are you discriminated against?' The fur on the back of Vo's neck bristled with indignation.

Petey jumped back, scenting Vo'so anger, his own fur standing up.

'I never said that. Prices are tough. C...c...competition is intense. And tourists spend more money.' His voice came out high-pitched.

Li-Pen put her hand on Petey's shoulder, meaning to comfort him. He jumped back as if she had hit him and cowered against the van. 'Don't hurt me please.'

Li-Pen's mouth dropped open and she gaped at Vo-Nam. 'We mean you no harm, Petey. We offer only friendship. Forgive us if we offended you.' Vo-nam said bowing, apologising for his wife's affront.

Petey peered out through his crossed elbows, which he'd used to protect himself. 'You want to be friends?'

'Yes, of course. You are like us. We know what it is like to be Di-Nuk.'

Petey dropped his arms away from his head. 'You do?' He stood there staring at them in turn, then shrugged human style and climbed into the van.

'Well, see you around then. I have to head home now.'

Before Vo-nam or Li-Pen could speak, he fired up the van and drove away.

'Li?' Vo turned to his wife, wondering what she thought.

'Very odd behaviour. Let's go back to the hotel.' She turned around and started walking away.

Vo-nam twitched his tail. 'No. I will follow him.'

Li-Pen paused. 'What? Why?'

'Because I want to know what is going on. I want to see the real Earth, not this fabrication that has been foisted on me.'

Li-Pen's tail curled around her left foot. 'Vo, really...forget it.'

Vo-Nam's tail twitched faster. 'I cannot. You may accompany me or not.'

Li-Pen watched him for a moment and then shifted her gaze to the retreating van. 'Race you,' she said with a smile. Then she bounded off after the van, on all fours like a Nuk cub.

Vo lost precious time gaping at her behaviour. On Dianur she would not have behaved so, not without shame. Vo trotted after her, using his human gait. She was fast but he would not stoop to grovelling along the ground like an unsophisticated child. After a few minutes, he switched to his native gait and then when it became clear that he would lose them, he dropped to the ground and bounded after them. After a few minutes, he got a stitch in his side and slowed down.

The van puttered along the deserted streets and then disappeared from view. Vo paused trying to see where his wife had gone. Then he inhaled deeply catching her scent. He caught up to her, as she was standing in the shadow of a street lamp. Vo-nam smoothed the hair on his head and scratched under his sweaty arm. 'Gone?'

Li-Pen put her hand on his arm. 'Wait. He is going there to that building. See?'

Vo peered into the dark, his night vision not as acute as his wife's. Then he saw it, a Di-Nuk-shaped patch of dark in front of the building. The door opened and Petey slipped inside.

Vo squinted. 'Didn't he say he was living nearby but that building is in the zone.'

Li-Pen loped away and Vo was hard pressed to keep up with her. As she opened the door, he arrived too. Behind it was another door with what looked like a visa card reader controlling it. A sign above listed the classes of visa permitted to enter.

Li-Pen ferreted about for her visa card, separating it from his. 'Mine should work.' It did. Vo-nam knew his visa card wouldn't operate the door. His was not one of the listed visa classes.

'Wait here. I'll go and see.' She went to step through and, suddenly desperate, he flung himself through with her, tumbling them down a long flight of steps. An alarm sounded as he landed. Li-Pen pushed herself up and shook her head, dazed but unhurt.

'Run!' she said. 'Now,' she added when he did not move.

Vo-Nam wasted no time and sped off. He thought she was following him but when he checked over his shoulder she had not. Had she run in the other direction? It was too late to turn back. He would get caught by whoever came to investigate the alarm.

His pace slowed as his panic lessened. Vo tried to take in his surroundings. He had run mindlessly down a corridor and turned in random places. As he gathered his senses, the smell hit him—a thick, offal smell, mixed with sweat and filth. It staggered him.

Holding his arm over his face, he came out into a larger space lined with balconies. Here the voices and the sounds intruded and intertwined with the stench. He kept running, not feeling safe in these alien surroundings. There was no air, no natural light. He was underground. There were people in here, crammed in, flowing over the balconies, dropping their waste, their food scraps. Some hit him as he ran and he wiped at the detritus, desiring to stop and clean his pelt. How he hated to be dirty.

He found a corner and sunk into it, keeping his eyes to the thoroughfare. Breathing through his mouth, he panted, letting his heart slow its excited beat. He tried to groom his pelt but it was no use. Only a complete soak would restore it. Forgetting about his personal hygiene, he looked up and surveyed his position. There were creatures here all around him. They looked misshapen, inhuman and dirty. They talked, though, and he could understand them. Their clothes were rags and they carried bundles, shuffling to a conveyer belt to place them down. Vo's gaze assessed the space and the people. The smell took on a new dimension, overlayed with a sickly sweet smell. It made it easier to breathe but he wondered what it was. No one had noticed him yet. What would happen if they did, would they turn him in? What punishment awaited him? Would they send him home? Well they had already decided that his stay was short. What more could they do? That thought allowed him to relax.

After he caught his breath, he climbed to his feet and went up to one of the beings. 'Excuse me, sir. Can you tell me where I am?'

The being ignored him and shouldered him out of the way. 'Please speak to me,' he pleaded to its back.

He turned to the next one and the next and all of them acted like he was not there. Then at last, a tall, rangy being came forward.' Your kind is not welcome here. This space if for Laots.'

Vo bowed his head. 'Thank you for speaking to me. You are familiar with Di-Nuk?'

The Laot shook his head. 'No, what I meant was that non-Laot are not welcome here. Find some other part of New London to inhabit.'

He turned his back, and Vo saw the scales on his neck and the strange ears. 'Are you part human, too?'

The Laot paused, hissed once as he turned around. Vo-nam's eyes widened as the creature puffed himself out, looming suddenly large. 'I could kill you for that insult. No one speaks of the shame.'

Vo-nam sucked in a breath. 'Insult? Shame? Please explain what you mean. I am half human and proud of it.'

The Laot stepped up to him and sniffed once or twice. 'Maybe you are. Why would you own it? We are refuse, mistakes, fodder. Why would that make you proud?'

Again Vo-Nam struggled to make sense of the Laot. 'I don't understand,' he said, feeling close to panic. The walls seemed too shrink around him and he could not quite block out that these beings were working, and working in terrible conditions.

The Laot beckoned him over to a small alcove out of the way of the Laot working. He lowered himself to the ground and gestured for Vo-Nam to sit beside him. Gingerly, Vo lowered himself to the ground, trying not to inhale the pungent odours that assaulted his nostrils. 'Not sure where you are from, Mister Di-Nuk. One of the many places humans went to find their answers, I would guess.'

'Answers? Do you mean the colonial offspring?'

The Laot gaped at him and then grunted. 'Offspring?' Then he laughed heartily. 'You think you are offspring, natural born like? Hah. They created hybrids for a purpose. They wanted compatible tissue.'

Vo-nam stroked his chin, his ears twitching. 'You make it sound that you were created in a laboratory. In my case, I had parents and grew up with tales of Earth.'

The Laot's eyes widened, showing red and blue around the vertically slit irises. 'Rubbish. Complete rubbish. All were laboratory grown and the tales you were told are rubbish too.'

'No. Not possible.' Deep down the seeds of doubt were planted. 'Why are you living here on Earth?'

The Laot put a cup on a small burner and heated it. 'Too many questions. Time for you to leave.'

Vo-nam stood, finding the being's manner difficult to interpret. 'Forgive me. I meant no offense.'

The Laot sniffed once and scratched the back of his neck. Vo caught sight of a brown bug slipping into his dirty shirt. 'Suppose you don't, I guess. Find your way to the next enclave and you'll work it out. Fine educated specimen like yourself.'

Vo frowned. 'How many of us part humans are there?'

Laot sucked in a breath. 'How am I supposed to know that?' Then he sunk back against the wall and appeared to sleep. Vo-nam waited for a moment and then crept away.

Throughout that day, he saw many different iterations of hybrids, felt his uniqueness slide away. There were humans, too, living in amongst the enclaves. They smelt and were thin and lifeless. Not what he imagined, not fat and happy like the off-world human tourists.

A small hunched over creature stopped to stare at him as he passed through a section of the enclaves. 'What do you do here, stranger?' it asked boldly.

Vo-nam halted, surprise making his tail twitch. So far none of the various hybrids had bothered to talk to him or note his passing. 'I am lost.'

'Haha. Heard that before. Not seen the likes of you around here. You must be one of them newer hybrids, born and raised off world from the smell of you.'

'Yes, I am a Di-Nuk from Dianura. I do not understand. What do you mean newer hybrids?' The creature had patches of grey fur on weepy pink skin. Vo found it quite repulsive and did his best to hide his distaste.

'I am an old reject. They used to bring us here and change us. But there were too many mistakes, too many rejects. Then the activists protested and the humans had to do their experiments off world. Only successfully compatible tissue was allowed to reside here.'

Vo-nam shuddered. 'Compatible tissue? I don't believe you.' Vo-nam did his best to cling to the remains of his shattered dream and failed. The world he wanted to belong to did not exist.

The creature shrugged and walked off. 'Nutter!' he called back before scampering up a ladder leading to a balcony. Vo-nam kept walking. He saw none of the fat, happy humans living in the enclaves. As he saw the decay, the despair, the twisted shapes of well over a hundred hybrid species, he began to believe. As he traversed the enclaves, he heard the chatter, pulled the threads of truth together.

The humans had filled this place with a multitude of hybrids, alien cultures, and fused them until they no longer resembled their original species or cultures. Then the humans went off world to make new homes, leaving their refuse behind them. Now on the surface, it was only the tourist resorts, sucking the money from the gullible and presenting a façade for the rest of the galaxy—pristine fakery, depicting a nostalgic past that probably never existed. But here, down here, this was where the real world existed—where the work was done, where the rejected hybrids eked out a pitiful existence. Vo-nam spluttered when he let those thoughts take root. He tried the stifle the sobs, but could not. Like the stench of the place, the truth could not be ignored. Staggering on, he found another enclave and then another, coming around in a large circle.

In a market, he thought found the source of meat that Petey had been selling. This type of animal was unrecognisable but Vo had his suspicions. When he allowed them to gel, he ducked into a corner and vomited. He suspected the malformed creatures were bred and slaughtered for food. How could he tell what the original species were and how different from the sentient hybrids around him?

The enclaves and the enclosed space started to overwhelm Vo-Nam. He wondered if it was best to hand himself in, best to end this putrid escapade within the bowels of the homeworld. Then he recollected that he had not seen anyone in uniform, not one human official at all. He wanted out but that would mean tracking his own scent and back tracking. It took a long time to return through the various enclaves, even though he bounded on all fours, disregarding the social niceties by ducking and weaving around the workers and those lingering in the passageways without so much as an apology. Yet necessity drove him. Too much, too fast, it threatened to corrode his sanity. He thought back to the pre-flight education program depicting Nuk being shot in the corridors of Old London, supposedly overwhelmed by the subterranean surroundings. His experience put a new gloss on that story. If they experienced what he did, then they were rational and appalled. Not insane or psychotic at all.

By the time he made the door, he was mired in fatigue. There did not appear to be any sign of Li-Pen. Nor was there anyone official there, ready to catch visa jumpers like him. He squatted for a while, trying to clear his head so he could detect Li-Pen's scent. At last he could smell her, he tracked her away from the door and then back again. The trails overlapped. Did that mean she had returned to the hotel? Was she there on the other side waiting to let him out? He shouted by the exit. No one came to investigate. Li-pen was not there.

Vo stood there gazing at the door, wondering how he could leave again. If he tried the door would that gain him anything except maybe setting off an alarm? He thought he had to risk it, even if they arrested him. What did it matter he had no more a place here than he did in Dianur. Vo-nam found that realisation quite shattering. All their money gone, all their goodbyes said and now this—a dead end.

Then he heard footsteps and quickly slunk away to the shadows. It was Petey, rucksack on his shoulder, using his visa card to open the door. Vo called out. Petey's head snapped around, his mouth agape. The door opened. Vo leaped forward, grabbed the visa card from Petey's hand and pushed past him to bound up the stairs. More alarms sounded but he kept on going. He heard the other Di-Nuk shout at him, yet did not understand the words. Vo-nam was breathing hard as he exited. Quickly looking around him, he threw the Di-Nuk's card back down the stairs. Petey grovelled for it. Vo loped away on all fours, glad to be clear of the stench and the crowding. He ran, and ran, through the pastures, dodging sheep and then he lay down and stared at the shimmering atmospheric dome above. Rolling in the grass, he rubbed the dirt and grime from his pelt. Then as he sat there grooming himself with his claws, he let his thought run. He was safe. He was free. He did not belong anywhere. No, he argued with himself. He had a wife and they would rebuild their lives, earn more money. Perhaps they could adopt a child. Li so wanted children, but their hybrid bodies could not produce compatible ova and sperm. They were effectively sterile as a couple. But there was a glimmer of a future there. What choice did he have?

After dark, he made his way back the hotel. No one challenged him or even appeared to take note of him. The authorities had not come to arrest him. That was a relief. He allowed himself to relax as he rode the elevator to his floor. Once inside their room he saw signs that Li had been back. The credit cards were on the bed and a message light was flashing on the side table. He stumbled over to it dumbly, realising that something must have happened. She should have been here.

Vo. There is no way to say this gently so I'll tell you straight. I am not coming back to Dianur with you. Earth has granted me citizenship and I want to stay. My uterus is useful here. I can breed babies for this company and they will pay me very well. And you know we could never.... I am sorry Earth is not what you thought it was. There are other places, better places. Don't look for me. Go back home, find a Nuk, and settle down. Sorry I've taken all our money to set myself up here. Had no choice. Sorry.

Vo-nam crouched by the bed and replayed the message he could not quite believe. A healthy female could carry four to five foetuses at a time. Technically, she could produce many litters of humans if her womb was compatible. Vo tried not to think about how Li-Pen had got her visa, maybe not because she had more human DNA at all. Then he recalled how she had been absent from the observation deck when they arrived. How she knew things like the new immigration rules. Perhaps that room with the humans and the catering.

It was her usefulness and compatibility that was the issue. He knew he had more human heritage than her, but he was not useful to them. He didn't matter. His humanness was a farce, created through lies and illusions.

50

He was one of many colonial conquests, a residue of earlier policies, ones that Earth would like to forget about, like they had the hybrids in the enclaves.

The room's buzzer sounded, then the door opened before he could give permission to enter. Armed men in uniforms barged in, swinging the door open with a bang. Vo-nam's hackles raised and he growled, instinctively on alert. One of the men stepped forward, as the others kept their guns trained on him, a small card in his gloved hand. 'Is this your visa card, Mr D'abela?'

Vo's tail swung from side to side. 'Yes. I must have dropped it.' Li-pen had held his visa card. She had had it when they entered the enclaves. His gaze slid to the bed, where the other cards were. His was missing.

'Yes, you did—in the enclaves—a place where you should not have been. Come with us now, Mr D'abela. I am afraid your visa has been revoked. Once your deportation has been processed you will be escorted to the next available ship.'

'Deportation?'

'Yes, you will be ineligible to return to Earth or any of its colonies. Do you understand what I am saying?'

Vo nodded. He understood too well. The final link was broken. Vo-nam swallowed once.

'Yes. I understand. May I wash first. I am so dirty.'

'No time for that. Come along now.' The man placed cuffs on his hands and pulled him along. As they shuffled him out the door, he tried to resist. 'But my wife has gone missing. Can you help me find her?'

'Come along quietly sir. We will see about your wife later.'

***

Vo felt the sting of the needle in his arm as the relaxant poured in. For a moment, he thought he saw Li-Pen in the cubicle next to him but then the image faded. His last few days on Earth were torture. They had kept him locked up. No one would answer his inquiries about his wife. Vo had many hours to think about robot sheep. Although he reasoned that he was not like the Laot, an experiment gone wrong, he still felt the taint of being part human. It would take time to find out the truth and maybe he never would. There was too much layering in the bureaucracy, too much politics and hiding of history. More and more, he understood the Nuk attitude toward him and wished that he had never come to the homeworld. It was hard to find pride and superiority when your self-worth had been expunged. On Dianur, he would finally understand his shame, his taint, his place.

Li-Pen had found a place on the homeworld but at what cost? She was useful, but would she be treated as a person, granted the same rights as others? That was no longer his concern. The divorce notification had reached him two days ago. It was over. What would he do when he returned home? He chuckled to himself as the meds loosened his self-control. Run on all fours and chase tasty *hunin*. Yes, he laughed, thinking about the taste of fresh killed meat. As the stasis unit hummed to life sucking away his consciousness, he wondered what robot sheep tasted like.

Author Note

The idea for this story came to me while travelling in the UK. The countryside was so green and lush, so perfect. As I looked upon the sheep that seemed so clean I wondered if they were robots and that it was all a show. I also have

English heritage and I felt a sense of entitlement when visiting. To me it was like coming home. Also, around that time, I read that scientists had been given permission to mix human and animal DNA and, of course, it's a post-colonial story.

Night of Masks and Spears

On Two Moon World, tribes gather for the making of men and women. While one moon hides its face and the other smiles, shedding its blue light on the land below, we gather at the great meeting house. It has been this way since we left the old world and spoke the one tongue. Now we are many tribes and fight among ourselves.

Why come in unity to live divided? Maybe the knowledge will pass to me when I fashion my spear and become a woman.

As I walked the path to the great meeting house, I listened to my grandmother recite the tales of old, of kin long dead, of those who rode in the white ships to bring us to this place. I nodded as she reiterated strictures on what a woman should and should not do. Usually, I found grandmother's voice soothing, particularly when she lectured me. Until we reached the base of the ridge, where the Melu village hung in the mist, I had been lost in my thoughts, letting grandmother's words fall around me. The shrill voices of the Melu women—their welcome words cutting through the air—set my heart beating. The men's voices, deep, rhythmic and booming, maintained my heart's new pace, unsettling me, making me sweat. The men thrust the sound of piercing spears and war chants into the women's welcome song, mingling in the mist.

Grandmother stopped talking as the climb steepened, focussed on each shove of her foot into the black mud. Gnarled hands clung to the branch of a Kakini tree as she pulled herself up to the next level. While assisting grandmother onto a terrace, I spotted a blue speckled feather in the undergrowth and darted away to capture it. The wind was blowing through the leaves, wafting the smoke from cooking fires down upon us. I scampered after grandmother and showed her my feather when she paused for breath.

'Another Kiku feather for your spear, Upai. What a mighty spear you'll make. But be careful—too grand a spear and a warrior will choose you instead of you choosing him.' Grandmother laughed, a wheeze between clenched teeth as she resumed her climb.

I smiled. My mother had bequeathed me another Kiku feather. Rare, beautiful gifts from a bird we did not kill or eat. Now I had two and my spear would be very special indeed.

As grandmother had to go first, with the chief, the rest of our tribe waited for us. She is the granddaughter of Lopai, the greatest of all Lelu chiefs. She was not a man, but she had his blood, and so did I, and we would honour the old ways. I walked with grandmother ahead of the rest.

'If your father were alive, Upai, his privilege would be to take you to your making. He would walk with pride ahead of the Lelu tribe.' The sound of determined, heavy steps thumped behind us. I stepped back. Uncle Taku shoved branches and people out of his way as he came to stand with grandmother, his mask scowling over his left shoulder.

I shivered at the sight of his mask, its mouth fixed in an angry growl and eyes a menacing glower. Grandmother's mouth turned down, and she turned to walk ahead without acknowledging him. As we walked with our tribe behind us, the men of the Melu village gathered in front of the village gates. Spears were shaken and challenges issued.

Our chief, Mukeni, answered their challenge. The Melu men began to dance with bodies hidden behind their long elongated masks, painted to fill their enemies with fear. I edged behind my grandmother, ashamed of myself for being such a child and allowing fear to take root in my belly. Every time we had a gathering, I had nightmares about the masks. I hated them, so much so that I did not know how I could marry a man who had made such a monstrosity. It was as if the masks reached out to me, pulled at my soul and sucked me dry. I cowered behind my grandmother to lessen the intensity of their presence. I pretended I wasn't doing it, because I knew grandmother would slap me. Luckily, uncle's presence made her so angry that she did not notice.

Uncle Taku, the man who could not take my father's place as chief of the tribe. I did not know why it was so. No one spoke of it. My childhood questions had fallen on deaf ears.

When the formal ceremony was over, I was free to mingle with the other girls. As a group we eyed the boys who would become men, singling out the ones who were not blood relatives. One boy caught my eye. I knew him from my childhood. He lived with us once for a few months. Bene was his name, and he had the most stupid grin on his sun-darkened face. I found myself smiling back at him before my grandmother called me to her side.

After a feast of fish baked in palm leaves and vegetables, we entered the great meeting house to sleep beneath the masks of our ancestors. I stayed close to grandmother, hoping she did not notice my fear. We spread a blanket beneath Lopai's mask, which was the largest and most fearsome of all the masks I had seen. I kept my eyes averted and tried to shut out Lopai's presence. For here was where I had to show myself, in front of my kin and the gathered tribes. There we sat while the elders chanted, argued and then their voices faded into the haze of fatigue. I kept my eyes from the walls, yet I could feel the masks pushing at me, pulling at me, trying to drag me into them. Bene was two bedrolls down; I chanced a look at him and he waved. Above his head, the mask Tukanku growled, mouth opening and closing like a monster from the deep of the sea. The mask's eyes showed mostly white, like he was seized by rage. I turned away and buried my head in the blankets. I felt myself shaking and tried to stop it. Grandmother would not tolerate such behaviour. She accepted my visions, the strange things that I could see, as she accepted the lack of curl in my hair. Grandmother expected me to deal with it, as a daughter of a great chief should.

Something startled me awake. There was nothing but the sound of many breaths exhaling and the occasional grunt and snore. Torchlight flickered over the mounds of bodies beneath blankets. I looked up and saw Bene's smile. He waved, urging me to follow him outside. But the masks were alive with hate. They writhed out from the walls, trying to snare anyone who passed too close. They whispered to me. I threw off my blanket, careful not to disturb my grandmother, and stole out of the meeting house. I dodged the apparitions that projected from the masks. The whispering grew louder, insistent. I chanced a sideways look and saw a mouth moving, heard words forming. I paused for a moment, realising that I had not heard the masks speaking before.

The words were hard to discern. It sounded like the one tongue. No-one spoke the one tongue anymore, though it was used in sacred ceremonies. My grandmother had taught me the words, though what I could hear was only vaguely familiar, distorted and meaningless.

One Moon's face was full, casting bluish light all around. I caught sight of Bene crouching in the bush at the edge of the village. I was tempted to turn around and go back to bed, but the thought of the masks changed my mind. Here, at least, there was a moist breeze to wash away the stale smoke. Bene's smile reached me and then he was gone. I sprinted to where he had been and followed the trail he left. He hadn't gone very far when I came up behind him. He crouched down and peered through some branches. Seeing the flicker of firelight, I crawled to where he squatted. In a small clearing was my uncle Taku. He was stripped to a loin cloth, his legs and arms streaked in blood. His mask lay on the ground before him. I heard him chanting as he rubbed what looked like small finger bones into the inside of his mask. Some of the words he uttered made my skin chill. It was the one tongue again. I understood the words, hate, vengeance, darkness. He pronounced them like grandmother. I could sense these feelings rippling through the air around him and could almost taste it. I watched carefully, realising that he was putting those feelings into the mask.

A tremor shook my hand. I did not want to see this. I did not want to be there. Masks were men's business and what Taku was doing was very wrong. Yet what I saw made me understand what I saw when I looked at the masks. Something in this ritual tied the warrior's spirit to the mask. All the aggressive tendencies were channelled and then infused into the carved and painted wood.

I tugged on Bene's arm and nodded with my head for us to leave. Startled, he released the branch and it crackled and shook. Leaves dislodged and floated down onto his dark hair. We both sat very still. Had Taku heard us?

There was no sound, just the pop and crackle of wood in the fire. Bene smiled and nodded. Before I could follow, I was grabbed and dragged into the clearing. Taku had his mask on. It danced in front of me, threatening, hissing. I edged back.

'What did you see?' Taku's voice was hard and quick.

'Nothing,' I whispered, throat tight. My eyes darted around for Bene, but I could not see him. Had he got away? I hoped so.

'What were you doing there? Who were you with?' Taku's hand reached around my throat and squeezed. His mask filled my vision. I could hear it. *Treachery! I will take them all while they sleep. My men come. They come. Blood. Blood. Lust and power!*

Oh no, I thought. *He means to kill us all. I have to tell grandmother.* I felt my head ache as his hand tightened. Through the pounding of blood in my ears, I heard Bene.

'She's with me.' Bene stood unmoving and unafraid.

Taku rose, dropping me to the ground. He picked up his spear and circled around.

Bene smiled, but there was no trace of humour in his face.

'You! Traitor's child.' Taku said, his spear-tip moving close to my head. 'You cannot have her. You're not worthy enough for one of Lopai's children.'

I blinked, remembering Bene's story. His mother had run off with an enemy warrior and his father had killed himself afterward. That was why Bene had stayed with us years ago. Our village asked that he be sent to live among the Melu, because he reminded them of his parents and their deeds and so he left.

'I have chosen her.' Bene said, standing very still. 'She has chosen me. Nothing else concerns us.'

Taku snorted. The mask angled toward me. I heard it sneer, growl and spit.

'I will take her first. Then you won't want her. She'll be shamed with her uncle's baby in her belly. At least the blood will remain true. Not watered down with the likes of you.'

Taku's words frightened me. He'd always watched me, waiting for me to undress when I bathed, peering at me from behind trees. Had he watched my mother in the same way? Grandmother said I looked like her, except for my forehead, which was strong like my father's. Was that why there was so much anger between them?

I lay on my back. Taku's spear pointed toward me. He angled the tip down to point between my legs. 'Move and I'll do it.'

Bene stayed still. I saw his gaze flick to me. I felt the spear tip and the brush of its feathers against the skin of my thigh. Already he had cut me. I felt the sting and the trickle of blood. Bene leapt with a sudden yell. Taku took his gaze from me and the spear wavered. I kicked hard, snapping it in two. I was on my feet, backing away. Taku and Bene circled one another, hands clenched and faces intent. Bene was empty-handed. Taku's mask leered menacingly.

I wanted to run away, but I couldn't leave Bene. His grin grew wider. *Was the boy mad?*

'I know what you are planning,' I shouted. 'You're going to kill us all.'

Taku's mask shifted toward me. 'What did you say?'

'I know what you are planning. Your mask talks to me. It told me of your treachery.'

Behind the mask, Taku's eyes widened. Bene's charge took him by surprise. The fastenings of his mask snapped and it fell off and into the fire. Taku lay in the dirt, shaking his head, dazed from the attack. Bene crouched in front of me protectively. My eyes shifted to the mask. It screamed. Flames danced over the macabre face, forking through the mouth hole and the eye sockets. It begged. The vision of its writhing mouth, the sucking feeling, dissipated. The mask was well alight. It sizzled and spat but it no longer whispered to me. Taku sat in the dirt, shaking his head. He blinked at us and to the mask, his face paling. Without a word he levered himself to his feet and lurched into the bush.

Bene walked up to me and grasped my shoulders. 'Choose me.'

I stared at him, his face composed with no smile there to make him vaguely silly. 'I will if you promise me something.'

Bene smiled. 'What?'

'Promise me you won't make a mask.'

His eyebrows rose. 'Without a mask I am not a man and cannot have you.'

I reached up and touched his face, liking the feel of his skin. 'I see things others cannot. I see that the masks are alive, even though their owners are dead. I see the unnatural evil in them.'

'Can I not make a mask at all?' He gestured to where Taku's mask lay blackened and smouldering.

I shrugged. *Who was I to stop him becoming a man?* I could only advise him. Yet I could not choose any man with a mask.

'That choice is yours. I urge you not to make a mask that is angry, vengeful or evil. Do not put yourself into the mask, or the blood of your enemies, and do not call on the one tongue to link your soul to the mask.'

I turned away, leaving Bene staring at the dirt. If he wanted me, he had to make a choice. I would not choose a man with one of those masks. I could not, but I did want to choose Bene.

When I crawled back into bed, I saw a few other girls returning to theirs. We exchanged smiles. Mine was feigned. I roused my grandmother and told her what I had heard from Uncle Taku's mask. She was the head of the house. It was her duty to deal with it. She got out of bed and went to wake our chief. I went to sleep. The night's activities had exhausted me and I had given my cares to my grandmother. The meeting house was alive with writhing masks, hissing and spitting at me it a strange rhythm. Sleeping was the only way to escape.

The next morning grandmother said nothing. Uncle Taku was nowhere to be seen. I trusted that my elders had dealt with any threat and I felt free of worry. I went with the women and we fashioned our spears. I found a strong pole of wood and smoothed it. Grandmother gave me a greenstone spearhead, freshly sharpened. It was her legacy. My finished spear was far superior to the others. No other has such fine stone, no other had two Kiku feathers. Although I was proud of my spear, I did not look forward to the evening. The boys, who had become men, would dance. I did not want to watch them. I would not choose.

Night was pierced with the light of One Moon. A large fire burned, reddening everyone's skin and casting dancing shadows. The boys, who were now men, came out, their masks freshly painted. I saw the angry faces, the snarls, the evil glares. I stood back and lowered my spear. I was going to walk away, but then I saw it. A mask, painted red, with lines around the eyes and a mouth stretched in laughter. My heart stopped.

Could it be Bene?

The other girls were pointing and jeering. I stepped forward and placed my spear at the feet of the man with the laughing mask. Before I rose, Bene had it in his hand.

'Beautiful spear, beautiful woman,' he whispered in my ear. 'But I will never scare our enemies away with this mask.'

My smile was very wide and I felt tears in my eyes. He had been clever. 'But they will think twice when you show them my spear,' I whispered back.

Bene laughed out loud and we danced.

Later, as we ate the feast and the elders blessed those who had chosen masks and spears, grandmother came up to me. Her face was sad. I remembered what I had told her in the early hours of the morning and understood that she had kept the news from me to avoid spoiling my happiness.

'What you heard last night, Upai, was not a plan for attack on us, here and now. The mask spoke of a deed long ago. It spoke of betrayal and anger and bitterness. It spoke of the murder of your parents.' Grandmother sucked in a huge breath, swallowing emotion. 'He killed my son. He killed his brother.'

Hot tears spread down my cheeks. All the angry looks and mutterings from my past came together. I saw how it had been. Bene put his arm around me and held me close.

Grandmother frowned. 'At the time, we suspected his guilt in their deaths but couldn't prove it. That is why he was never made chief. I spoke against his choosing. I spoke against my own son.'

'Has he fled?'

Grandmother shook her head. 'No, Taku is dead. He knew that you spoke truth, that you had heard the mask's words, the words of his own soul. He could not live with it any longer. What was burned in the mask returned to him. He could not bear the guilt, the shame.'

'I am sorry, grandmother.' I hugged her.

'There is nothing for you to be sorry for. If not for your gift, I would never have known for certain. The suspicion has eaten at my soul all these years. Now I can let it go. Now I can heal.

'When we confronted him with the truth, Taku confessed. Once free of the secret, he became more like the boy I once knew and loved. I think he will bathe in the light of the two moons with the rest of our departed kin.'

She walked away, her swaying gait reminding me of her voice and the comfort it gave. I danced with Bene, feeling free and loved and happy. I had chosen a man with a special mask, one not filled with hate. It gave me hope that one day we could live in harmony, that one day we would rid ourselves of fear.

Later as I lay with Bene beneath the stars, I saw grandmother creeping through the village. In her arms she carried Lopai's mask. She chanted in the one tongue as she threw it in the fire. I said goodbye to my great, great grandfather's spirit as it dissolved among the flames.

This story came to me while I was sleeping at my sister's flat in Randwick. There were wooden masks on the walls, masks from Fiji, Papua New Guinea and maybe a tiki from New Zealand. They gave me bad dreams.

Warning Buoy

Evie felt consciousness returning while she was still deep in slime. She resisted the urge to breathe until she had surged out of the life support fluid and wiped the synthetic mucous from her nose and retched, dislodging the dregs of it from her throat. Her eyes were out of focus, but she could tell straight away that something wasn't right, something was missing. It was Sam. He always emerged before her, programming his unit that way so that he was there to help her untether the tubes and the intravenous drips that had kept her sleeping for their jump. By the time she had pulled herself out and extracted the last tube, she saw that he wasn't still interred in his own life support. Nothing appeared to have malfunctioned. He wasn't dead, which had been her first fear. What was it then?

After a shower, she stood and shaved her head in preparation for their next outing while thinking back on the time before the jump. They had finished maintaining the beacons on Bright Star station and made love with the light of the system's star before heading below to go into deep sleep. Sam had been full of joy, for no particular reason other than he loved working alone out here in space, just to the two of them. Perhaps it was his capacity for deep thinking while he stared out the viewport that had first attracted her. That and his silence.

She keyed the intercom. 'Sam?'

A few moments of crackle and then Sam came on line. 'You up already? Dinner is almost ready.'

'You weren't here.'

His breathing sounded over the intercom for a bit and then she heard him whisper. 'I know...' before he cut the connection.

Drawing her brows together she began to mentally catalogue plausible reasons for the 'mood'. It was obvious he was in one. By the time she made her way up to the command deck she was over it. She smiled crookedly at him, which encouraged him to embrace her before he slapped her on the back and said, 'Time to eat.'

'Yeah, right...eating,' she said anchoring herself to the small table. He refused eye contact and that made it difficult to broach the subject of the 'mood'. Her eyebrow lifted. 'Do you have any more of that Pinot Gris? I could do with something to wash your cooking down.' She could do with something to wheedle the issue out of him too.

While went in search of some wine, she gazed out of the view port, dragging up details of their next maintenance stop. Out the view port she saw them—two gaseous nebulae, one more distinct than the other. The fainter one was a dying star, feeding the newer, hotter, brighter one. She tapped her finger on the table, ignored how the smell of Sam's cooking made her stomach roil and recalled the name of the mission. 'Tolstoy Patches,' she said to herself, nodding. It was a newly marked corridor, with top-of-the-range transponder buoys. They guided traffic between the nebulae, warning ships away from the hi-alpha emissions, fluctuating gravity and other flotsam and jetsam caused by star birth. Space bent sharply on the other side of Tolstoy Patches, giving ships the required run into the nearest wormhole.

Sam arrived with the wine. She wasn't officially on duty until the next morning so she could drink the whole bottle if she wished. For herself, the wine was more for washing the salty cum metallic taste from her tongue. Not much to be done about the odour in her nose. It took a week for the solutions to wash out of the system. She guessed the pay was worth it. She and Sam could retire quite well if they worked another ten years at navigation aid maintenance.

'Fascinating,' he said, watching her stare out at the nebulae. 'That is a microcosm of creation. The old made to new. Elements broken down and reformed. The universe adapting to change.'

'It's very pretty,' she said with a smile.

Evie didn't wait for Sam to finish unscrewing the lid, she had her glass aloft ready for the first splash. When they had finished the first glass, Sam was still uneasy and uncommunicative. It set her teeth on edge. Why couldn't he just tell her? But she knew why. The same reason they were out here on their own. The same reason they hardly took shore leave. He couldn't stomach life. Life with other people. The hurried, harried madness of the cities on Earth, or the impersonal and sterile existence on space stations. He just didn't gel with the rest of mankind. It had taken a year of service with him to break down the barriers he'd erected and nearly that long again to work her way into his overalls.

'So, love, what have you been up to? Been awake long?'

Sam frowned over his glass and took a long pull of the second glass. 'Been doing maintenance on the Work Horse.'

'Is there a problem with your Work Horse?' she asked.

'No...no problem...just maintenance.'

Some inner warning tickled her mind. 'Not enhancing it are you?'

The vague distant look in Sam's expression shifted. 'How about a warm chocolate and a nice massage?' The grin was wide, with no hint of subterfuge. Evie let it ride.

'You know how to woo a girl now don't you?'

***

The next morning she sat at the main station going over routine operations. Sam was below working on the Work Horse again. She hoped he didn't touch hers, as she hated surprises. Chuckling to herself at some fond memories of automated clutch arms coming miraculously to life, unexpectedly, she flicked through the comms register. It was there that she found the message. It at once angered her and explained what was going on with Sam. It was serious too. Not news he would take lightly, she expected. After Tolstoy Patches they were to return to base. Not for reassignment. No they were to be made redundant. The advance in technology meant that it was more cost effective to deploy automated repair drones.

She flicked off the message and continued with the pre-operation preparation, running routine diagnostics on the navigation buoys. Not only did she do bounce back signals to confirm their position in comparison to the deployment settings, she ran test of the frequency emitters to ensure they were broadcasting within specifications. Ships' crew could identify the location through the type of beacon and the broadcast frequency of the signal. The preliminary reports made her frown so she scheduled detail scans that would provide a better report within twenty four hours.

Sam came in, sweaty and smelling of ozone. 'Running tests?' he asked.

'Yeah just going through the routine.' She wanted to say 'get the fuck over it,' but couldn't. She wasn't sure she even wanted to broach the subject. But she had to somehow. There had to be away to get him over this hurdle. If she could see a way forward then he must too.

'What's for dinner?' he asked, slouching into a chair.

'Just slops, I reckon. I've been working.'

Dinner was awful and it wasn't the slops. He knew she knew and she knew he knew that too. How ridiculous! Evie had to star, had to allude to the issue. There had to be a way forward. 'Isn't there a space station being built? Do you think they'll need technicians?'

Sam shook his head. 'Not the same.'

'Geez Sam. Don't do this. Don't let it get to you. We can still be out here among the stars.'

He was shaking his head and avoiding eye contact, pulling into himself.

'You and me, we're strong.'

'No.' He floated away from the table and grabbed hold to the viewport. 'No. I don't want things to change and no lecture from you is going to change that. I will fight it.'

'Fight it? How? It has already been decided.'

'There's got to be a way. I'm going to find it.'

'I say we adapt. We find something else to do that suits us.'

Sam focussed on her then, the pale yellow ring around his pupils blending with the green and brown flecks. 'Adapt?' He rubbed his chin, an excited glint in his eyes. 'See you later.'

'Wait. We haven't finished discussing this. Sam. Sam?'

Evie anchored herself to the table and brooded while she sucked her coffee. She said interesting and derogatory things to her coffee about Sam, the universe is general and the difficulties she had had with the lifelong involvement with the opposite sex. 'Obstinate bastard,' she said loudly, wishing he could hear her in the Work Horse bay.

Sam was absent from his bunk that night and Evie, not quite sure how to deal with him and their situation went to bed alone, refusing to let thoughts of life after a career in navigation aid maintenance ruin her natural sleep. There was time enough for nightmares during unnatural deep sleep.

The next morning she reviewed the reports on the Tolstoy Patches navigation buoys and hurled a few more curses into the air. The reports didn't make any sense. Some of the frequencies were way off the specifications and two of the beacons were giving strange readings on the bounce back and that shouldn't happen.

She queried the ship's computer, Nestor, on the impact of the nebulae environment on the design parameters. Nestor needed to take some more readings before producing a report.

The blare of alert on the bridge shocked her out of her seat. Adrenalin surged through her brain as she went through the protocols. Asteroid hit, hull breach, systems failure. 'Sam!' she called over comms. 'We have an alert, Sam?'

All the systems checked out. But then she knew. Her gaze flew to the internal temperature readings. Sam. Workroom. Fire.

***

The air was thick with acrid smoke, drawn into the corridor through the vent. Her throat ached from screaming his name. Wiping snot and tears from her face, she struggled to stand. She couldn't bring herself to look through the small view port into the smoke-filled bay.

He was in the Work Horse all geared up and apparently prepped to go. Yet there had been some kind of power surge. He hung there lifeless. She banged on the door but it wouldn't open. Then as she peered helplessly though the view port she saw why. He had cycled the lock. His horse was on the arm in preparation for launch. His head lolled, as the unit jostled him. Debris preceded him out of the lock and then he launched.

Tearing herself away from the door, she headed back to the bridge. Nestor gave her his vitals, which confirmed what she'd seen. He was dead. Nestor was unable to override the launch of the Work Horse. Sam was gone. Just like that.

The two-man vessel was now a one-man one. A senseless ending, she thought as anger warred with grief. Even the next day, while she sat there with stale coffee on the table, a helpless, nothing feeling lingered. She knew why he'd done it. Knew why he couldn't go on. He couldn't adapt. Feeling superior was cold comfort. The memory of his body hanging there, in his rig, electrocuted returned again and again to haunt her.

On the bridge, the computer suspended it analysis of the navigation aids of Tolstoy Patches to concentrate on analysing Sam's accident. It was strangely quiet. No Sam chatting, breathing or just being. She glanced to the mess table. Spilled coffee looking like blood. Sam's blood.

With a sigh, she tried to shrug off the guilt, tried to stop herself from working out the little things she'd done or not done. The closer she nestled in the curve of the view port the more she felt surrounded by stars. She closed her eyes, hiding the hurt within. How could he have done it? Left this beauty behind him?

The console beeped sharply. Her analysis of the 'accident' was complete. Did she even need to look at it? Her gaze paused briefly on the readout. The image stayed in her mind, the words burned across her consciousness. It was true. He'd done it to himself. But he'd been careful and hadn't taken her with him. She didn't know if she was glad about that. She filed the report and sent it back to base. Let them digest that.

The numbness of grief was still upon her, only routine kept her going, kept her not thinking about him, the loneliness, and the thoughts about the waste of his life.

Sleep was an escape when routine didn't serve to take her mind off things. She slept through three shifts, leaving the computer to run things. What did it matter if she didn't eat or wash or read the reports? Who cared anyway? The company was folding, the high powered brass would be retrenched with large financial payouts. She'd be lucky to collect her leave entitlements. Cold coffee filled her cup, she sipped it, found it soothing. She idled over to the mission report readout. The unusual readings remained, in fact they were even stranger than before. Hastily, she paged through it. 'Confirm, nav report readings,' she instructed the computer.

Twelve buoys marked Tolstoy patches. Only nine responded to the routine bounce. Malfunction? The buoys were nuclear powered. They'd last for an age out here. What then? Sabotage? Theft? Now that they were closer, she instructed the computer to repeat the bounce, a tight beam signal to each buoy's transponder. She watched each signal return, noted the ninth one was weaker than previously. Heartbeats passed by, the other three didn't return.

'Are we close enough for sensors? I want to know if they are in situ?' she said to the computer.

Nestor's flat voice answered. 'Readings are ambiguous.'

'What do you mean, ambiguous? Either they are there or they aren't. Do it again.'

The computer went silent for ten minutes. Evie tapped her teeth with her finger nails, while she stared out the view port. Filaments of the nebulae reached out, dissipating into the far reaches of space, way beyond the confines of her visual window. She eyed the view port's filters and nodded. It was set for enhanced viewing, green, blue and red, the colour of the elements of life, hydrogen, oxygen and carbon.

The console chimed. 'Yes, what is it?'

'Only eight buoys register on the sensors.'

'But we had a bounce for nine before. Reconfirm bounce.'

She watched the returns. Only eight returned this time. She calculated her estimated arrival time, making adjustments for Sam's death. Her mind was occupied with the nebulae, perhaps there he would float forever. He'd like that or would have, his essence mingling with a new star system. She filed a report about the findings of the navigation buoys and sent it back to base. She'd be finished by the time they received it. Would there be anyone to read it? Who cared about a defunct navigation maintenance crew? No one, except her. She'd do her job. Anger rose up then. 'You bastard, Sam,' she yelled into the empty bridge. 'I won't give up. I won't.' The last choked off, and she was racked with a soundless sob. There was no sound for her grief. Only glowing filaments of nebulae gas to witness her pain.

The twin nebulas filled the view port. She was tracking to the entry of the patches, angling the nose of her ship for the centre between the first two markers. Detailed specs drifted across her screen. The readings from the first two buoys were strong and within specifications. Everything looked as it should. There were elevated high alpha emissions in the area and other cosmic rays spiking. She had the computer check them against the databanks. The buoys were there for a reason but she didn't know the history. Usually markers went up after a disaster, more like a memorial to lost lives and with the vain hope that it would spare others.

Now she was being sceptical, deprecating her reason for living. Her job was important. Servicing navigation buoys saved lives, ships, cargo and served navigation. That was a decent purpose. The reference to the disaster was in the system. A major passenger liner had blown up here. Its systems had scrambled, leading to the death of four hundred people in the cold of space. No, she wouldn't think about Sam.

'Move to next set,' she ordered the computer. A touch of thrust and the ship nudged forward, deeper into the channel between the two nebulae.

The next two buoys checked out okay and their anchors in position. The remainder, though, were emitting strange returns. Buoys seven and eight had stopped responding. Number five was weakening.

'Can you get us there any faster?' she asked the computer.

'The ship is already at maximum thrust,' answered the computer flatly.

'I'm going to prep the Work Horse for an EVA inspection. Let me know when we're near buoys five and six. I should be ready by then.'

In the utility room, she readied her unit. It was a bit of chore because its interfaces were quite intrusive. She had to insert tubes for collection of urine and tubes to go down her nose to her throat to feed her. Some of the units articular devices were hot wired into her nervous system, a bit uncomfortable but once she was hooked up, she could move like a ballerina amongst the stars, and she could affect repairs more efficiently than if she went in a standard suit. Her gear checked out. She started to re-shave her head, clearing the stubble. A clean scalp provided better adhesion for the units inserts. The unit beeped its readiness, all systems go, all food packed and all tools at the ready. She climbed in. The computer chimed in that they were closing to the eject point. Evie hurried the last of her preparations, scraping the inside of her nose as the tube went down. She winced as the saline drip went in and jostled the waste connector so that it slid into the stoma in her abdomen. When she moved, the unit moved. Lurching to the hatchway, she went through the final check lists. Her heart leaped excitedly, until the unit pumped her with a sedative. It didn't find her excitement compatible with its operations. While she was EVA the unit ruled her.

***

Clear of the ship, she stilled, savouring the first moments in space. It was like a rush of fear and awe, haloed with an overwhelming sense of insignificance. Her stomach adjusted to the zero gravity and then she could focus.

Nudging her Work Horse toward warning buoy five, she checked her readings. The anchor had loosened and the buoy was slightly off its co-ordinates. She fed the information back up the link to her ship. A nice lumpy bit of feedback for the design engineers, she thought with clenched teeth. The ship's computer didn't acknowledge. 'Nestor? ' But then she could see the outline of the buoy. Her Work Horse lights arrowed in, already revealing pock marks on the outer skin of the buoy. Hovering close by, she reached out. 'How strange,' she said, running her right articulator down the side of the buoy's metal facing. It was scarred, three gouges attested to that.

It was more than a debris hit. Either it was an impact or the molecular substance of the casing was breaking down. She looked around nervously. Something about the damage was creepy. Was there something out there with her? Immediately she cursed herself for a fool. If only Sam was here, she'd never have thought such an idle and superstitious thing.

Floating near the now malfunction warning buoy, she tried to ascertain the environmental readings that may have impacted on the buoy. She's have to write up a detailed report. Her sensors were hazy, too much radiation interference to gain readings more than a few metres away.

Her ship drew nearer, too near. Although it monitored her progress it normally didn't approach that close. Perhaps it was having difficulty with the radiation too. Turning her mind back to the buoy, she found that the inspection hatch wouldn't open. The buoy was not operating at all.

A shadow flickered as an object broke her beam of light. Her eyes widened and she immediately began to look around. Nothing. Suddenly, something whizzed past. She squinted, then flinched. 'Nestor?' she said through the link. 'Scan that. My sensors don't appear to be operating.'

Her heart leaped. The unit pumped some beta blockers, slowing her heart rate. It took a few minutes to get her breathing back to normal. Why was she so spooked? There was nothing out there, except the warning buoys. One must have come loose from its mooring.

'Nestor? Are you reading me?' No response. She switched to the emergency channel and faced the ship. It was close. She waved. No response still.

Shrugging off the ship's errant behaviour, she readied herself to burn through the outer casing of the buoy she was examining. She touched the metal where her torch had been aimed. The metal oozed strangely, dripping in slow globules, like blood from a wound. 'Now that's weird.

Computer, these buoys are standard steel-titanium aren't they?'

Silence.

'Ship? Are you reading me?'

'Yes,' came the response. Finally she thought. ' Radiation is interfering with communications. I am experiencing difficulties with normal functions.'

'Critical?'

'Uncertain. I have to interpret some new programming.'

'Programming? Err...keep me updated.' To herself she said, 'Why is this buoy melting? Geez.' She poked the finger of her articulator through the metal. It pushed through with little resistance. 'No wonder they aren't working.' That shadow flickered again. Pausing, she glanced around. The object careened into the buoy she was connected to, sending her and the buoy spiralling away in opposite directions. 'What the...'

Queasiness settled in as she rotated backwards head over feet so many times she lost count. Her thrusters allowed her to slow her spin.

Had that buoy attacked her? It could have been a random action, caused by the momentum when it split from its anchor. She had no idea which buoy was rocketing around the patches. The ship still monitored her. But unusually, the computer hadn't reacted to the incident. The patches were certainly living up to their reputation. Her leg jerked, and she felt some pain, some pinching. Hovering there, she wondered what to do next. Was there time to salvage the remaining buoys? Did she have sufficient gear to leave a temporary marker? She wished Sam was there. At least she could bounce ideas off him. Her arm felt itchy. She needed to scratch it. Perhaps it was time to go back to the ship and think about what to do next.

'Nestor, I'm coming back in. Prepare a temporary warning buoy and record the following message. 'Warning, warning, Tolstoy Patches are unmarked, repeat, unmarked. Suspect unusual amounts of radiation may affect metals and shipping. Minimal sensor capabilities. Warning, warning....''

A blast nearby made her somersault backwards again. She found it hard to stop her spin this time. Her movements were sluggish, her equipment unresponsive. Her ship span in and out of her vision. After repeated tries her thrusters fired, allowing her to hold her position. 'Did that come from the ship? Nestor, acknowledge.'

The computer was silent. 'Computer?' While she watched in dismay the ship started gaining speed, jerking to the left and right. It seemed drawn to her. She powered her unit, trying to get away. This is crazy, she thought. She tried sending a manual code through the uplink. She needed to kill the engines. The touch pad dented when her articulator fingers tried to punch in the digits. Panic filled her gut. This time the unit didn't compensate with drugs. She was on her own. The ship stopped abruptly. Perhaps the code made it through after all. She gazed at the dripping, pock-marked touch pad and shook her head. 'Computer, acknowledge. Kill the engines,' she yelled. 'You have to retrieve me. The Work Horse is starting to fail. I repeat Work Horse is failing.'

Instead of responding to her hail, the ship careened downwards, spiralling down and down. Evie had her mouth open. Then she cringed, seeing nothing but white as the ship exploded. Debris swung into her, sending her spiralling.

Of course, the ship was affected as were the buoys and her Work Horse. Why hadn't she seen it sooner? Now, there was no ship, no way home. How or why seemed meaningless now. This was it. Hanging there in space with debris floating around her, Evie sucked in breath after breath, each one feeling harder to draw in. It was as if she were too fat for her unit or it too small for her. Her workhorse harness constricted her breathing, pulling tight across her chest.

'Warning, warning...' her message began to repeat in her ear.

'No, this is crazy.' How did her message repeat when the ship was gone? Had everything she'd been through made her hear things? Her message mustn't have cleared the buffer.

Her unit tightened further, another worry for her. She felt the implants delving, like ice fingers digging, pinching, groping. Panic took over. Her scream of fear drowned out her message. Either her machine was breaking down irretrievably, and she had only moments to live or the machine was taking over—no merging with her. God no!

'Warning, warning...' her message looped again. Her throat was hoarse, but she no longer cared to scream. There was no point. Her unit began to speed up, rocketing through the Tolstoy Patches, blaring her warning. She had no control and the ice claws in her skin penetrated painfully.

Evie felt her mind drift and cool and slow. She thought of Sam out there, his essence part of a new star. Right then, she didn't know where the workhorse stopped and where she began. Her ears were filled with the sound of her message. She started to feel drowsy, felt the now warming metal slide into her veins through the implant. 'Warning buoy,' she whispered, the irony not lost on her. Her eyes were closing...but there was another Work Horse drifting into her vision. It was moving.

'Sam?' Her mind struggled to stem the creep of metal. Hallucinating, she thought vaguely. Then she heard it. Sam's voice repeating her message. Sam's rig floated in close. It was his body, but not him. The metal of his rig, webbed over him, like veins. 'Warning, warning...'

At first, her reaction was horror and fear. She'd end up like that. Sam drifted closer. His eyes weren't dead. Some power glinted there between the webs of metal. The machine oozed liquid metal like a tail. Yet there was Sam, animate. Had he known? Had he led the way for her to follow? Was this the 'adapt' he was thinking of when she spoke to him last? Was there hope and not despair in his thinking.?

Oh Sam! Dare I believe? Is this where we end and begin again?

Her eyes closed as the last of the metal slid into her veins, becoming as blood. She was conscious but altered. Alive but no longer breathing. Neither death nor evolution did she fear. The silence of the stars still soothed her. Sam was there and he was ready to adapt along with her. Eyes glowing in the darkness around her. The message she'd sent kept on blaring.

Warning, warning, buoy. Warning, warning buoy.

Author Note

This story came from a number of places. I was doing an audit of the management of the Australian navigation aid network and through that I learned that warning buoys, lighthouses etc are usually put there after disasters. So immediately I started thinking about outer space and what if there was an accident etc. Then, also the lighthouse keepers had all been outsourced and replaced with automated beacons or contractors and that made me a little sad. I think being a lighthouse keeper would be a kind of calling. About the same time, I was doing some reading about nebulas, particularly nebulas that are growing as they feed off another one, possibly a dying star. And then it just gets a bit weird.

Lake Absence

Miles locked his cattle in the stockyard every evening. He counted them to make sure none could roam. Four calves, eight cows and one old bull huddled together safe behind the sturdy fence. Turning, he gazed across the barren, wind-swept basin of land over to his small farm house—a crumbling old house, built by his father.

The pale sun set and the brown night encroached. Miles hurried to complete his chores. At the well, he pumped out thick muddy water and washed his hands. The aroma of the evening meal wafted on the dry, dusty air, teasing a restless groan from his gut. Closing the door on the lengthening shadows, he kissed his wife, Belle, on the cheek and asked her how her day was.

As she spooned out the turnip and barley stew, she told him about the grinding of grain, the baking of bread and the dryness of the well.

'Surely it won't be long,' he said. 'We'll have water again soon.'

'I hope so,' she said, 'Otherwise we'll have to drink the cows' milk.'

Miles laughed. 'And what will the cows drink?'

Catching his eye, Belle laughed too. Yet underneath it all Miles tasted the worry, the despair, the constant wondering what if.

The next morning Belle was up before him, leaving a cold hollow in the bed. The sun had not yet risen. He heard her there, stoking the fire so she could bake bread. Miles lay there with sheets tucked up to his chin while he mentally prepared himself for the day ahead. Then he felt it. The dry air moistened within the space of a breath and a soft, cool breeze tickled his exposed skin.

The clink and clang of Belle stoking the fire ceased. 'Is that?' she asked in a whisper from the kitchen.

Miles threw back the covers, surged to the window and flung open the shutter. It was still dark outside—he smelt the dampness in the air and heard the soft lap of gentle waves.

'I think so.'

Belle came up beside him. 'I wonder why there was such a long gap this time. There doesn't seem to be any way of predicting it. Would be so much easier if we could.'

Miles fingers scraped against the bristles on his chin. His shave would have to wait. Events now dictated his chores for the next few days.

As the sun rose, he and Belle stood on the shore of the lake. Yesterday it had been barren plain, pockmarked with grassy nodules, now it was full to the brim with pale brown water. Assorted bits of flotsam were visible bobbing on the surface.

'I'll go East and start foraging,' suggested Belle. 'I can pop back and keep an eye on the bread.'

Miles nodded, scanning the large lake. 'I'll check the well and fill the dams and then start on the West side.' He moved off and then paused. 'Must let the cows out first and milk them.' He headed off, knowing he would not see her again until well after sunset. If he was lucky he'd catch a glimpse of her in the kitchen when he brought in the milk and set it to cure.

Some hours later, essential chores done, Miles grabbed some rope and headed along the shore. In places, he noticed that the lake exceeded its usual boundaries. Picking up branches, and odd cartons, he stacked them in piles on the dry embankment. He continued to walk around the water's edge, eyes carelessly drifting to the short choppy waves that so fascinated him.

He caught sight of a brown thing floating a few feet from shore. With a frown, he waded out to see what it was. The closer he got the more afraid he became. It was Kaylen's best cow, drowned. Miles cast his gaze around looking for his burly neighbour. Perhaps his own foraging had not taken him this far around the lake yet.

Kaylen did not count his cows when he shut them up for the night. Without Kaylen to witness how he found the cow, Miles was nervous about touching it. Usually cantankerous, Kaylen had bordered on irrational since his wife died the previous year. Yet looking at the cow, he knew the longer it stayed in the water, the greater chance of losing the meat to spoilage.

Miles tied a rope to the cow's head and towed the bloated carcass closer to shore. Puffing with exertion, he took off his hat and wiped his brow and then stilled. A shadow fell across him. 'What are you doin' with my cow?'

Kaylen circled him, his harsh brows drawn over deep-set eyes. Miles stepped back. 'Saw it out there, drowned. Thought I'd bring it ashore before the meat spoiled, and then I was going to come over and let you know.'

Kaylen was nodding. 'You killed my cow.'

'No. I was walking along looking for firewood and saw it there.'

'So you be saying. I say you killed my cow. What you going to do about it?'

Miles swallowed. 'It drowned. Nothing anyone can do about that.'

'Replace it.' Kaylen's fists clenched and he leaned in too close.

Miles backed up. 'I can let my bull service your other cow.'

'Definitely. We'll see about the rest. Wait here and I'll get the cart.'

Miles wanted to get on with his chores but he couldn't up and leave that would make matters with his neighbour worse. No point in making bad blood when there were only two families living by the lake now.

When Kaylen was out of sight, he explored lakeshore, picking up twigs and branches and floating bottles and stacking them in neat piles on the shore.

Soon, he heard the rusty grind of Kaylen's cart and his neighbour came into view.

Together they dragged the carcass onto the bed of the cart. Miles helped push the cart back to his neighbour's house and tried to leave. He had much to do to secure the flotsam before the lake disappeared again.

'Help me hang it in the shed,' Kaylen said, using straps to secure the beast to his back. With a sigh, Miles helped to lift it, groaning under the weight of the beast and they got it under cover.

Miles wiped sweaty hands on his trousers. 'I really should be going now. Got to get back to my chores.'

'Fine, you lazy bastard. You'll get nothin'. What will Belle say with no meat to feed that babe in her belly? All you had to do was a little bit of work.'

Turning his back to Miles, Kaylen pulled a long knife from the wall of his shed. Then he sat to sharpen it on the whetstone.

Emotion roiled within Miles. How did Kaylen know that Belle was pregnant? He must have been spying on them, listening through the windows.

Miles shivered at the thought. Looking at the carcass, he had to admit that they did need the meat to supplement their diet. A freshly drowned cow was not spoiled meat. He rolled up his sleeves.

Kaylen slashed the hide around the hooves and around the neck. Miles grabbed the fore hooves and held the carcass so that Kaylen could slit the beast down the middle.

Offal spilled onto a groundsheet. Together, they sectioned up the animal and laid it out in the shed. Nothing was wasted. All of it was useful from the ripe flesh of the rump to the intestines. Miles wished that the work progressed faster and hoped Kaylen would not insist that he stay for the salting of the meat and the cleaning of the offal. He'd be lucky if Kaylen spared him a bone for all his hard work.

Long hours passed and thirst plagued Miles. 'Have to get home and have a drink and a bite to eat. If you need help, let me know and I'll come back.'

Kaylen grunted and continued with his task. He did not look up as Miles headed out of the shed and back to the lake.

Although Miles was tired, he took his time to pick the shore clean as he made his way home, after washing the blood from his hands.

Concern wrinkled, Miles' brow. There was no way to avoid telling Belle about what happened. She wouldn't be happy as there would be twice as much to do the next day.

Soreness in his muscles weighed him down as did the knowledge that it was going to get worse before better. As he walked under a starless sky, he saw the horizon glow with pale yellow light that imbued the night with a brownish cloak. The outline of a few dead trees reached out, clawing the air. He stood there, letting the lap of water and the ghost of sky surround him. It was then he heard the moan.

Stopping his breath, Miles listened for the sound to repeat. There it was again. Near the base of a partially submerged tree. He scrambled over to it. In the dark shadow of the roots was a man shape.

'Who is there?'

'Awwwwl,' said the man shape.

Miles felt gingerly in the water and touched a hand, which in turn grasped him. Carefully as he could, he half dragged the man and laid him on the shore.

Miles ran his hands over the man's body and could feel no broken bones or obvious injuries. That was a relief. If he had broken skin or bones then there wasn't much they could do but watch him die. They had no medicines here. All had disappeared when the others went away. Not that there had been many people or medicines to start with.

Leaving the man lying in the dirt, Miles went to lock his stock in their pen. Then a final check of his chores, he returned the lakeshore. The man lay still and quiet but came to his feet readily when Miles dragged him up. Together they lurched to the farmhouse, the man barely consciousness.

Miles began to worry about the stranger. Miles couldn't anticipate what argument there would be but Kaylen didn't need an excuse to pick a fight these days. Best he hide the man until he recovers and can fend for himself.

With the light behind her, Belle waited by the open door, flicking sparrow-sized moths that dived bombed into a pan by her foot. They were nice fried and served with yoghurt.

'What have you found?' she gasped as she ran toward him. Hands to her mouth, she gaped at the man.

'A new kind of lake salvage, I think. Quick let's get him inside.'

In the wan candlelight, the man's complexion appeared grey. Twigs, leaves and dirt clung to the remains of his charred trousers and three or four rips in his shirt revealed pale hairless skin. Thick brown, pungent mud covered his sturdy boots. With eyes clenched tight, the man moaned slightly but did not open his eyes or speak.

'How did he get here?' Belle's voice had a hysterical edge. Her hand covered her abdomen.

Miles soothed his panicked wife, cupping her face and smoothing the concern from her mouth with his thumbs. 'I don't know. We have to hide him somewhere.'

'Hide?' Her puzzled gaze cleared. 'Oh I see,' she said nodding. 'That would be the best thing. The wood closet under the floor is near empty. We could put him there for now.'

Miles raced into the bedroom and found the edge of the trapdoor. Belle stood by the man, steadying him with a hand on his shoulder, her gaze returning repeatedly to the front door. After lifting himself down into the small hole, Miles cleared the left over driftwood and then levered himself up again to find a blanket. Belle helped as best she could in sliding the man's semi-inert form over to the hatchway. Then they lowered him feet first into the hole. Belle then cut up some bread and a filled a water jug to put beside the man in case he woke up.

A thump on the door made them both start. Miles nodded to Belle, who walked over to the door while Miles eased the trapdoor closed, and followed behind her.

As the unlocked door swung open, Miles saw Kaylen standing there filling up the doorway, a joint of meat on his shoulder. 'Here you go, little missus,' Kaylen said in his rough voice. 'Thought you could do with some meat in you, seein' you are in the family way.'

Miles ground his teeth. Belle cringed away from Kaylen, unable to hide her fear. Ever since Kaylen's wife died in childbirth the year before, Belle had been wary of their neighbour. Belle had tried to help at the premature birth, but there was nothing she could do. It was a night of blood and death.

Kaylen smiled broadly and stepped through the door as Belle cowered away. How Miles wished Kaylen would follow the others and move away and leave them in peace.

'That's mighty generous of you,' Miles said stepping forward. Kaylen ignored him and thumped the meat onto the table. Miles nodded to Belle, who went to bring glasses. 'May we offer you some wine?'

'I recall you have some very nice spirit hiding around here. The one your father laid down.'

'I think we have some left.' Miles cringed. He wanted to keep that aging spirit as long as possible, savouring for the anniversary of his father's passing. He went to the pantry and pulled down the small botte. Kaylen would not leave until it was all drunk.

Belle stepped forward and placed some plain biscuits on the table before their guest. She eyed the small cups as Miles poured the spirit in. 'I'm feeling tired. Do you mind if I go to bed? I have to get up early in the morning to start the baking.'

'Don't you go runnin' away on us,' Kaylen bellowed. 'Sit down and have a drink.'

Belle lowered her head. 'Thank you for the invitation but my mother always said a woman should not take strong drink when carrying a babe and it has been a long day.' Before he could speak again, she slipped into the bedroom, shutting the door quietly behind her.

'Bah. What a weak woman you have there. Always skulking around and hanging her head. Got no life in her at all. In these parts, a man wants a woman who will work beside him, drink with him and fight with him. None of this 'feeling tired' and popping off to bed as soon as company comes along.'

'Take no offense. The babe does tire her and the worry with the lake and all. We were well short of water before it filled again. It's a woman's nature to dwell on things.'

Kaylen swallowed his cup of spirit in one gulp and slammed it down. Miles refilled it again, wishing he was better able to deflect their neighbour's unwelcome attention. 'My Amy was a strong woman. She didn't let anyone talk her down. Not even me when I was giving her a whooping. I miss the old girl.'

'Ever thought of going to town and looking for a new wife?'

Kaylen raised an eyebrow. 'What and bring one of them soft things here to the lake? Incredible. The things that go through your mind. Suppose you and your missus have been hoping that I'll go there and not come back. I'll be dying here. Tell you straight. Nothing will make me leave this land. It were my father's and his before him. I promised him, I did. That I wouldn't leave.'

Kaylen put his cup down for another drink. Miles poured it in. No longer drinking the strong, smoky spirit himself. There was not enough to fill Kaylen's cup.

'You're a bit light on in the drink.'

'That's the last. Sorry.' Miles yawned widely, not really working hard to feign his fatigue. He would have to tend to the meat before bed too. Kaylen lingered for another hour, sometimes staring into space and not bothering to speak. He filled up the small cottage with his presence and his scent. Miles could only sit politely and wait for his neighbour to grow bored and leave. Miles didn't realise he had dropped off to sleep until Kaylen scrapped back his chair and stomped on the floor boards. 'Terribly sorry. I was more tired than I thought.'

'Ah, you be weak. Weak like your wife.' Without any further word, Kaylen flung open the door and staggered out. Miles rested his back on the door after he shut it. Kaylen was right. If he were stronger, he would be able to stand up to that bully.

All was quiet in the night. The stranger did not stir and the night sounds consisted of soft lapping waves and the occasional lowing of cattle.

After losing a whole day with the cow and the stranger, Miles thought it best to get up and start his chores early. He trod carefully outside, skirting the lake in the wan light, picking up driftwood and other materials. As dawn broke, he carried the bundles of wood back to the house and went to milk the cows.

Miles had his head down as he walked, thinking. He looked up and stopped suddenly. The gate to the cattle pen was open. Immediately, he suspected Kaylen's hand. The loop of rope that he used to secure the gate hung on the post. At least, Kaylen hadn't cut it.

One cow remained in the pen. He turned around. No cows were near the lake. With water there, it was unlikely one would accidently drown. Whistling he called to his cows and was delayed until well after breakfast rounding them up. His bull and a calf were gone and he guessed Kaylen had helped himself.

Miles chewed his lip as he headed into the house. Kaylen was unlikely to return the calf, no matter what tactics Miles tried.

Belle did not look up when he came in and she put the food down in front of him without speaking. He heard her sniff as she turned away.

'What is it?' he asked.

Swinging around, she glared at him. 'You ask me that? Why don't we move away from here, away from him? He controls us, plays with us.'

'You exaggerate. It's not that bad.'

'Really? We have a stranger hidden in our woodpile because we are too afraid of Kaylen to be open about him being here. Instead of telling him to go home last night, you let him drink all your treasured spirit. What else has he done?'

'Done?'

'I can tell by your face that there's more.'

Miles lowered his gaze to the crumb-covered table. 'He's taken the calf. The bull is missing too and he let out the cows. That's why I'm late for breakfast.'

'Oh Miles. This can't go on.'

'I know, I know. Any sound from our guest?'

'Not a peep. Will you check him before you go out? Make sure he is still alive, as I don't want to working with a dead body in the house.'

Miles finished his bread and broth and went to the bedroom. He opened the trap door and peered inside. The man stirred, blinking and shielding his eyes from the light.

'Morning.'

The man sat up. Miles reached down and extended a hand. The man looked at it, grabbed it and climbed out. He eyed Miles, then his gaze went to Belle standing in the doorway. He nodded to her.

Belle smiled and waved him to the table. There she placed fresh biscuits and hot tea and stood over him while he ate. The man's gaze wandered around the room and then out the window. After eating, he moved closer to the window and stared out at the lake. Miles stood next to him and pointed. 'Found you in that.'

The man nodded and resumed staring out at the lake. Miles was wondering what to do. Did the man speak? Was he from the town over the hills? How did he make this far on foot?

'The lake. How did you get in there?'

The man turned toward him, eyebrows furrowed. 'Lake?'

He words were slow and accented. 'Yes, the lake. Water.'

The man mumbled to himself. Miles tried to discern the words he was speaking but could not. Then man sat down again and put his head in his hands. Belle reached over and touched the back of the man's neck. 'Fever,' she said, snatching her hand away.

'I'll put him back below. You move away from him. It could be catching.'

'Well it's too late now seeing I already have touched him. Best we check him for injury. It could be an infected wound.'

Miles urged the man into the bedroom, then mimicked taking off his clothes. The man nodded and then peeled off the remains of his shirt and then his trousers. Across his lower back were three gouges, like claws had shredded him. One of them was inflamed and oozing pus. Belle was right.

Belle boiled some cloth and came into the room to tend the man. Once the wound was cleaned and dressed, Belle gave him one of Miles's shirts to wear and then he returned to the woodpile without argument. The stranger was asleep before the trapdoor lowered. Miles left Belle with her chores and went out to do more foraging. Before he could return, he had to face Kaylen and retrieve his bull.

Miles made good progress with the junk that he collected. He found a half buried box of canned food;

various lengths of twine; a metal bucket; some bottles of what looked like wine; floating glass balls, which would make a nice gift for Belle, and various lengths of cut wood along with more drift wood. There were bits of paper floating on the surface of the lake, which he scooped up. Dried they could be useful though any text on them had blurred and smeared. Further out a container bobbed on the light waves. Miles rolled up his trousers and took off his shoes so he could wade out and grab it before it floated away. After a few hits with a stick, he was able to guide it into range. This container contained shirts and other items of clothing. They made Miles think of the stranger, so he carried them to shore and, after putting his shoes on, carried it straight home. His stomach rumbled so it was time to eat anyway.

He heard Kaylen's voice before he reached the front yard. Quickly he hid the container behind the outdoor wood stack. Then he rushed inside.

Belle hunkered close to her stove, hand clenched on her stirring spoon. Kaylen was a few steps away from her, hands on his hips. 'Why don't you come and sit down with me?'

He could hear Belle's reply. 'I told you. I'm very busy. I don't have time. Please leave me alone.'

'That is not very neighbourly of you—'

'Can I help you?' asked Miles, stifling his anger.

Kaylen turned slowly. 'No, if I wanted to talk to you I'd come looking for you. I wanted your pretty lady's company.'

'Well, she is my wife. It isn't right that you come here when I am away from the house.'

'Not right. Who says?'

'I say.'

'You say. Who are you to tell me what to do?'

'Last time I checked I was Belle's husband. It is my duty to protect her. This is my land, my home. You are only a visitor here.'

'Visitor? Not guest?'

'Not a guest when you enter uninvited.'

Kaylen turned toward him, drawing himself up to his full height, anger staining his face red. Before he could direct his anger, Miles jumped in. 'Now that you are here. I wanted to ask you if you have seen my bull today? Somehow the gate was open this morning...'

A look of surprise transformed Kaylen's angry expression.

'Don't be askin' me about it. You're the careless one to leave the gate open and let your cattle stray. Not my fault they are a wanderin'.'

Miles slammed his hand down on the table. 'I did not leave it open. I shut it every night as well you know.'

Kaylen's gaze raked Belle, who stood shivering by the stove. 'What business is it of mine to know your habits? I'll be off then seeing I'm not welcome in this house.'

'About my bull. I'll walk back with you and fetch it shall I?'

'What bull? There is only my bull and my calf.'

'You lost your bull last season. Come on let's not argue like this. Come along and we'll talk about it as we walk back to your place.'

Kaylen grunted. Belle's face had gone pale. She looked ready to swoon. Kaylen glanced at her and grunted again, setting his feet in motion to the door. Miles stepped back and allowed him to pass, his heart beating frantically in his chest. He had stood up to his neighbour? Had it worked?

With one last glance at Belle to check she was all right, he followed Kaylen out of the door. What was going on? Did the arrival of one stranger set things out of balance so much? As Miles walked, he wondered if they would find equilibrium again.

Kaylen stalked back to his farm without saying a word. In his stockyard were Miles's bull and calf. In a corner was also some of the salvage that Miles had collected the day before. Kaylen had helped himself to it. Kaylen saw him noticing and lifted his chin, daring Miles to speak of it.

Miles walked up to the stockyard gate. 'Thank you for finding my bull for me. You may keep the calf.'

Kaylen grunted and said nothing as he watched Miles open the gate and lead his bull free. Miles knew the other man did not deserve the calf, but thought it best to quieten the argument.

With a nod to his neighbour, Miles led his bull back to his property, further lamenting the lost opportunity to gather salvage from the lake and tackle his chores. With the bull safely in the pen, Miles irrigated the garden and collected more of the previously collected and stacked salvage before Kaylen could steal it.

Night came early and cool, teasing the air with soft puffs of mist rolling in from the lake. Tendrils drifted over the cottage, mingling with the smoke from the chimney fire. It was warm inside the kitchen. Belle bustled about moving pots and shifting plates. The stranger sat at the table, complexion looking healthier. The man stood when Miles entered and smiled.

'I thank you for the help,' the man said slowly and with an accent.

'You're welcome. What shall we call you?' Miles's gaze slid to Belle. She seemed perfectly calm and happy. If Belle did not fear him then all the better.

'I am Wayfour. In all my time riding the rift I have never heard of Lake Absence.'

Belle turned to the table placing bowls of stew and hot flat bread in front of them. So Belle had been talking to the stranger. 'Riding the rift? What is that?'

'I ride the rift between the lands of Ictual and Laden.'

'I have not heard of these places. They are not the lands divided by the lake.'

'No, not the same thing. I speak your language although your version is rather strange. So I think your people must have come from Laden originally, possible accidently like I have.'

Miles shared a look with Belle. She smiled weakly and then drew up her seat. 'So we are in a land between these places you travel,' he asked the stranger.

The stranger shrugged. 'This is not a normal land. Do you understand? This is a between place. A place that only exists because of the rift. That's the only way I can explain it. The water...I mean the lake, is part of the process, part of the balance.'

Miles sat back and blinked. 'Not a normal land. What do you mean?'

'When I say I travel between the lands I do not speak of ordinary travel, like on foot or by boat. Ictual and Laden exist on different planes. A great machine generates the rift and to travel from one place to the other one must ride the rift. It is hard to explain, if you have not seen the machine, or the rift.'

Belle reached out and squeezed Miles' hand. 'Wayfour's a rift rider. When one travels on the rift, the water comes here and when they return it goes away again. Not many take the journey anymore. This explains why the lake is so unpredictable these days.'

Wayfour dug into his food. After swallowing a mouthful, he said, 'Belle has explained the situation here. I will keep out of sight until I am ready to ride the rift again.'

'When will that be?'

'I am weak still. A day maybe two.'

There was a clunk outside the door. Miles and Belle started. It could only be Kaylen again. With a nod to the stranger, Miles stood slowly while the stranger darted into the bedroom and slunk down into the woodpile. Belle moved Wayfour's plate and hid it behind the pot on the stove as Kaylen swung the door open.

He walked in without saying a word. Miles was frightened by the wild look in the man's eye.

'Evening neighbour. What can we do for you?'

'What's going on here?'

'Going on? I'm just having dinner and a chat with my wife.'

'I heard voices, a stranger's voice.'

Belle stepped forward. 'Miles was telling me a story and putting on a stranger's voice. Won't you have some stew? I have plenty here.' She held a bowl out to him. With a swift cut of his hand, he knocked it flying.

'Don't want no damned stew. I want the truth. Who is here?'

'No one I told you. You can't just come in here and throw your weight around.'

'Who says I can't? I am doin' it aren't I? You goin' to do somethin' about it?'

'Calm down, please. Just calm down. There's nothing to get upset about.' Miles backed away, his hands making placating gestures.

'Really?' He lunged for Belle, grabbed her to him and tried to kiss her. She struggled in his grip. Miles started shouting but didn't know what to do. He tried tugging his wife out of the other man's hands. Kaylen grabbed her left breast and squeezed. Belle screamed and struggled.

Miles jumped on Kaylen's back only to be shrugged off. Kaylen backed Belle onto the table, smashing the bowls that were there. He started hiking up her skirts.

'Stop!'

Kaylen paused. 'You want to be tellin' me what's goin' on now? Or do I fill your wife with my seed because I can?'

Belle was weeping now as she tried to keep her skirt down and push Kaylen off her.

'I told you nothing is going on. We were eating our dinner.'

Kaylen shoved a struggling Belle back hard. She hit her head on the table. Kaylen began to fumble with his trousers. Miles picked up a shard of pottery from the floor and readied himself to launch at his neighbour. Before he could act, Belle aimed her clawed fingers at his face. Kaylen backed off her with a cry, hands going to his eyes. 'Filthy bitch. I'll get you for that.'

Kaylen shouldered Miles out of the way and lunged for the door. Miles stunned, stood there gaping, until the sound of Belle's weeping reached him. Then shaking himself, he went to comfort his wife. When she quieted, he shut the door, wondering what would happen next. The stranger Wayfour stood there his face glum. 'I see what Belle means. I hate to cause you all this trouble.'

'The trouble would be greater if he found out now. After that row. He'd probably kill you for being here.'

'If you are well, I will rest now. Perhaps I will be fit enough to leave tomorrow.'

Miles nodded. The trapdoor lowered and he led Belle to the bed. She would not talk to him. Miles did not blame her. What kind of husband was he that he could not stop another man trying to rape his wife? Kaylen's loneliness must be hard on him. When his wife was alive, he was more bearable.

Miles lay on the bed but couldn't sleep. Worry harried him. If he did let his eyes close, the scene with Belle pinned under Kaylen kept replaying.

Belle continued to keep to herself, not huddling close to steal his warmth. Disgusted with himself, Miles shuffled out of the house to start his chores early.

The door of the woodpile lifted as he trod to the kitchen. Wayfour climbed out and placing his finger to his lips, signalled for silence.

It was dark outside, with dawn many hours away. The sky was sickly yellow with brown-stained clouds. Wayfour accompanied him to the lake. Copying Miles, Wayfour stopped to pick up wood and other odd bits and stack them as Miles did.

'You do not have to stay here. I could take you back with me.' Wayfour spoke after a while.

'No,' Miles said as he squatted to tidy a stack of wood. 'This is my home. This is all that I know. This thing with Kaylen will pass and things will go back to normal.'

'Are you sure? Belle said she wanted a normal life for her and her child. Will you not consider it?'

'What leave here? Leave our home?'

'You can make a new life. A life where you belong. A better life too. Not one filled with toil.'

The dawn broke and dull light spread over the dun coloured lake. 'Best you return to the house and hide yourself. Kaylen could be abroad at this hour.'

Wayfour nodded, cast his gaze around them and the left. Miles hurried to his chores, hoping to put his sleeplessness to good use. Why did Belle talk to this man about her fears? She should talk to him? He did not like the talk of leaving. This was his world, his home, his life. He rejected the thought of leaving.

All the salvage was neatly stacked and the cows milked before he headed back for breakfast. The stove was cold. Belle was still abed. The stranger was up. When Miles came in, he handed him some cold bread.

They both looked towards Belle and then shared a look.

'How do you feel?' Miles asked in a whisper.

'Better. I think I can manage to open the rift. You should come with me, both of you.'

Miles shook his head. 'Thank you again for the offer. But this is the only life I know. My father built this house...'

The stranger nodded slowly. 'It's too dangerous for you here, dangerous for her. I won't push you but I will show you how to trigger the rift. I will wait for you on the other side for a few days before moving on, in case you change your mind.'

Miles nodded. When the stranger was ready and had said his goodbyes to Belle, Miles checked the perimeter to make sure Kaylen was not anywhere around. Together they skirted the lake. The stranger walked slowly, pausing every now and then. Miles pointed to the tree where he had found the stranger.

'That is not the point. I drifted there. I need to feel my way. Not easy to detect if you don't know what you are looking for.'

Wayfour continued on and then slowed. He appeared to be sniffing but that wasn't it. 'Do you feel that?' he asked Miles quietly.

Miles drew up closer. At first, he felt nothing and, then as he relaxed, he felt a slight vibration in the air. He glanced at Wayfour who nodded. 'We are close. Come along. I will show you and then you must pull back otherwise you will be drawn into the rift.'

The stranger led the way. All the time Miles could feel a vibration that made his hair lift. The stranger stopped.

'This is the point. I will need to step into the water here, maybe twenty paces. Can you feel the change in vibration here?'

Miles nodded. Together they strode out into the lake. At twenty paces, Miles felt an increase in the vibration. His teeth ached. Wayfour made him move around the point to show him how to feel the exact trigger point. True to his word, Miles found that only at that point was the feeling the strongest. Then the stranger explained the trigger. Miles doubted him. Could such a thing be so easy?

'Goodbye Miles. Come to Laden if you can. Forget this place. Your people were trapped here by mistake. There is no future here. When the great machine stops working, which it will one day, I fear this place will disappear.'

Miles gaped at the stranger, finding his words hard to understand or believe. He waded back to the lake's edge and then watched as the lake disappeared along with Wayfour. He stood there for a while contemplating the empty lake bed, with its pools of stagnating water. Could this place really be some kind of refuse heap, the sludge of another world, occasionally flushed as a stranger transited across worlds through a rift? No stories told of these things.

Belle was up and cooking when he closed the door behind him. He stood by the door waiting. She kept working. Casting his gaze to the ceiling, he sighed. 'He's gone.'

Belle nodded and put a bowl of food on the table. It was a soup with bones in it and root vegetables. He sat down to eat. The aroma made his stomach grumble. 'I'm sorry, Belle. I should have acted sooner.'

She sat opposite him. 'I'm afraid. He will not forgive us, forgive me. We have to go now before it's too late. If not through the rift then we must follow the others over the hills to the town.'

Miles took a mouthful of soup and swallowed. 'Leave here? You're serious.'

'Yes. If you will not take me, I will go alone. Wayfour told me how to find the rift. I will not wait for that beast to come here and rape me while you are milking the cows or...'

'Or what?'

'Standing by and watching.'

'Belle!'

'It's true isn't it? You could not stop him. He could kill us both if he wanted. That man is evil. We must get away."

'It's not that bad.'

'Oh Miles. Can't you see? It is that bad. What if he comes when you are out? You can't even try to stop him then.'

'Tomorrow. Let's talk about it tomorrow. I'll think on it. Yes, you'll see I will think of something.'

Belle's eyes were dark as she lowered her head to eat. They ate in silence.

The next morning Miles was up again before sunrise, outside with his chores and rounding up the cows for milking as the sun rose. Today he would make butter as enough cream had soured. The monotonous chore would calm him, calm his troubled mind and let him think about Belle's words.

He worked solidly until hunger drove him back to his house. Smoke did not rise from the chimney. Belle must still be feeling poorly.

The door was ajar when he approached the cottage.

'Belle?' he called out, seeing there was no laundry hung to dry. The water buckets by the door were still empty. There was a strange smell in the air as he stood on the threshold. After being out in the sun, the room was dark.

'Belle?'

The room was quiet and still. A pot was on the cold stove. A slice of bread lay separated from a loaf on the table. Frowning, he stepped through the room and stood on the threshold of the bedroom. Blood puddled on the floor, a trail of dark stains led from the bed.

He raced over to the bed, heart thumping. Belle's clothes were shredded and torn and a large puddle of blood and gore sat on the sheets. Miles cried out and then bit his fist.

'Belle?'

He wanted to cry and to whimper and bewail his heartbreak. Kaylen had killed his wife. Then he saw Kaylen behind the door. Blood leaked from a head wound as he moved into the light. Kaylen's eyes glittered with anger and madness. Miles jumped back, fear warring with anger. The smell of blood, perhaps the remains of his unborn child lay in front of him. Why could he not find the strength to stand up to Kaylen?

Watching him silently, Kaylen lifted up his hand. The blade of his butcher's knife caught the light and Kaylen let out a roar.

Miles dropped and rolled. The knife came down, and down, thumping against the floor boards. There next to the door was a cooking pan. Belle must have used it. Just in time, he deflected a blow from the knife with the pan. Scrambling to his feet, Miles aimed high, thwacking Kaylen in the side of the head. The larger man stumbled back.

Miles turned and ran, then stumbled. Kaylen's knife sailed overhead, giving a whistle as it cut the air.

Kaylen's heavy tread followed behind. Miles went for the closest tool he had. He threw the empty water bucket and then went for some wood. There a few steps away was the axe. Kaylen roared again.

Miles lunged for the axe and swung. Kaylen grabbed it and they fought over the handle. Kaylen's hand bled and then his grip weakened. Miles pulled the axe hard to the side and used the momentum to convert it to an overhead swing. The axe hacked a chunk out of Kaylen's ribs. Miles dropped the weapon and ran to the lake.

Near the shore he saw the blood stains. Could it be that Belle lived? She must be heading for the rift. Behind him, he heard Kaylen roar. The blow he had dealt the other man had not been fatal. Kaylen was coming. He had to find Belle quickly.

On the dry lake bed, he saw Belle close to the trigger point.

'Belle wait!' Casting his gaze behind, he saw Kaylen closing in. He had gained ground, more ground than an injured man had a right to do.

Time was running short. He had to trigger the rift before Kaylen drew closer. If Kaylen was caught in the transition then he would travel too.

Miles reached Belle. She was barely conscious, crawling toward the rift as if driven. He helped her, grabbed her bloodied hands and lifted. She cried out. Blood stained her body and Miles could see the wound. Kaylen had cut her abdomen, had tried to cut the child from her body. Miles shuddered at the terror Belle must have felt during the attack. It was his fault. Why had he not listened? Why had he not acted when he had time? Now it was too late.

Miles calmed himself so that he could better sense the trigger point. He manoeuvred Belle until his hair stood on end, propping her up and whispering to her. There Miles stood at the centre of vibration and reached out with his mind. He felt the air shift around him, felt the slide of water and the tearing, sickening sensation as he moved. He heard a yell suddenly cut off, the sound of Kaylen being swamped by the lake.

There he stood, bright light surrounding him, on a plinth. Belle sagged to the ground at his feet.

'Took you long enough.' Wayfour stepped forward and touched Miles' arm. Then he saw Belle. 'What happened to her?'

Miles swung around, fell to his knees and screamed. The land around him was full of strange bright colours, the sky was a startling blue and in the distance were rigid and sharp-edged buildings.

Overhead, the sky roared with powerful machines. He panted as his panic waned and then drew into himself, finding a calm, quiet spot in his mind. His fear had to be controlled. Belle needed him. He turned to Wayfour, who knelt and stroked his wife's hair from her face. There was something tender and revealing in that touch. Wayfour spoke into a wristband, calling for urgent aid.

Wayfour looked up at him and nodded. 'Help is coming. She'll make it. It's not too late,' he said to Miles as Belle reached up to touch the stranger's face with blood stained fingers and curled herself toward his body to weep.

Confused emotions battered Miles. It's not too late, Wayfour had said. But as Miles watched he knew that it was. Belle looked to the stranger now. It was the stranger who had protected her, who brought comfort and hope. Miles had left it too late. The damage had been done. He'd acted too late. He'd lost it all. Lake Absence. His home. His wife. His life.

Author Note

Like other stories this came together from a number of places. Firstly, Lake Absence was inspired by Lake George, near Canberra, Australia. At the time it was dry but when I first came to Canberra it was full of water. It is a lake that has these weird cycles of wet and dry and I thought as I sat on the bus heading to Sydney: what if that cycle happened overnight? Then I thought of the kind of life that would be. The rest built up from there. That there was this 'no space' that was inhabited by people who everyone had forgot and here was Miles, trying to live on, not wanting anything to change. In this, he reminds me of the farmer who keeps to the land and suffers when there is drought and disease but still remains because that life is all he knows and understands. This story has not been previously published. I came very close (it was shortlisted for a semipro mag) but just gave up trying.

Other

I felt a tug when the medico-servo arm retracted as it completed repairing the worn lining in my wrist's uni-joint. The med-unit then extended a nozzle and sprayed synth-skin over the open wound to conceal the flesh and wiring. After it dried, the incision mark began to fade sparking a memory; not one memory, but countless ones, echoing into the past. Thin lines of blood tracing over skin, the fine scrapes of scalpel cuts, smells of blood, body fluids and antiseptics, all mingled and converged, like this moment was the focal point of my life.

Yes, I'd had countless medical procedures, cut after cut, hurt upon hurt, until my pain receptors were dead. I felt nothing, well almost nothing. I didn't know how many times parts of me had been replaced, the organic replaced with silicone, titanium and circuitry. It was too many times to count. From the moment, I, Devlin, had been chosen, there was no going back. I was stuck here until I finally ground to a halt. These machines, though, had been programmed so well they never let me be and I wondered if it would ever end. How long had it been? Two hundred and fifty seven years, five months and a handful of days since Sal said goodbye.

I flexed my hand, testing out the nerve linkages. There was a ping as I bent my thumb. It was just a tendon readjusting, metal grating over metal. I walked over to the viewport as I double-checked my arm movement. The plains of Tuemy filled my vision, the vast plains stretching to the horizon were uniformly flat. My organic eye looked out to the dark ruined remains of the Destratic continent.

It contrasted with the lighter, dirty-brown sky, a sepia rendering without the soft, creamy hues of light play.

The other eye, the scanner, displayed the topographic inclines and infrared in a mash of mauve, red and green lines and swirls.

My scalp prickled and the hair on my arms stood up. The air seemed to thicken and contract. I inhaled a quick short breath.

'Other?' I whispered, eyes scanning for a physical presence. Other had been with me on Halfen for some time and as real to me as my own mind. It kept me company.

The heaviness coalesced like a storm building. The hairs on my neck stood up.

'You...' the voice answered. I didn't quite hear it. The sensation was more than that. It was more like I felt it in my mind and my body. There wasn't much to hear on Halfen anyway. I lived on my own so what did it matter if my aural mechanism was faulty.

'Do you remember them?' I asked.

'Them?' asked Other. The strength of its response vibrated through me, jarring my teeth. Damn those osseo-integrated implants!

'No...' said Other after a space of heartbeats. 'Remember...what...they...did...'

A shiver sped up my spine, sending a crackle of static electricity snaking into my steel jaw. I licked my lips. My eyes flicked out the viewport. Yes, they had destroyed half of Halfen.

'I remember them...' I sighed, still haunted by the dream, the flashback to the real life I had once lived. Where there was love, people and her. 'I dreamt of Sal last night,' I said to Other, but mostly I spoke to myself. 'It was so vivid. Her smile cut through me. So close, so new, so real...'

I recalled the dream fragment. Me and Sal running through the fields of Tuemy. Not the blackened fields I could see out the viewport now. No, in my dream they were salmon-pink, the mousolis plants rippling, ever rippling, as far as the eye could see. I sighed again, remembering the taste of her.

'I love you, Devlin,' she said in her clear high voice. 'Make love to me here, right now. Let's be the first...'

'...remember...' Other's voice tensed, a clench of thunder. I lost the memory, the surreal past faded once again to lie muted in the feeble remains of my human brain.

'Oh damnation!' I shouted, fist balled, angry at self and Other's interruption. Coherent dreams were scarce now and memory defunct.

'You?' said Other, its voice slow and drawn out like the sound of granite, grating against granite.

'What's the point of remembering? It won't bring them back.' I turned away from the viewport and headed to the flight deck. There was no use in delaying any longer. I could feel coercion building within me as my sub-routines realised that I had not commenced duty yet.

'Come?' asked Other, its voice pitched slightly higher than a rumble. Other liked it when I went outside. It seemed to relax and sometimes I imagined it smiled.

'Yes...it is time.' I readied myself for the patrol, absently re-organising my gear and slowly checking my body for signs of decay, mechanical breakdown or wear and tear. I don't know why I bothered checking myself since the machines never missed much.

I struggled into the pilot seat and set off. First, a flyover of the Destratic continent, the dead remains of mousolis stretched from end to end. Then I flew across the Null Ocean, a brown-grey solution of acidic chemicals.

'Nada,' I said to my log. I'm sure there were thousands of reams of logs, stretching back through time with me saying 'nada, nada, nada, naught, nothing, zilch, and nada.'

Then I increased my altitude to 10,000 feet above the Sinastic Continent. A glowing plain of salmon-pink unfolded before me. There it was my reason for existence. It was like a beautiful virgin, desirable and untouchable. I frowned, completing my circuit and went back to base.

I wearied of this daily ritual, my patrol of the skies. There was never anyone there. My earlier zeal had worn thin through the years. Now only the programming embedded in my brain served to prompt me, when I couldn't even bother any more. I never thought I'd still be living like this after all this time. They left me and never so much as sent me a message.

That night I sweated through countless fragmented dreams of them, my fellow colonists and my wife, Sal.

'Don't do this to us, Dev.' Her words cut through the jumbled images. 'Say no. Don't stay here.'

'I have to. I told Stan I would.' I turned my back on her and heard her sobs. The plains of Tuemy were dark then. I felt like the plains, the conflict of duty and love, leaving me desolate, destroyed, alone. Sal loved me, accepted me, and I'd never given myself to anyone as I had to her. Even though the computer had matched us as we boarded the colony ship, our attraction had been instantaneous and powerful. The separation had left me hollow for years.

With me remaining on Halfen, Stan would have claimed her when they headed to their next destination. Stan's wife had died in stasis, our only casualty. I guessed I was the second. Compatibility scores were irrelevant when there were only two unpaired colonists.

The dreams of Sal were sent to punish me, I was sure, to remind me of choices that couldn't be undone and that I had lived too long and for a null purpose.

I sat up, not knowing why I was there, the reason lost in the decay of my brain cells. Those hard won memories and dreams retreating back to where they lurked. Sweat leaked out of the natural part of my skin. I felt clammy and uncomfortable.

I got up and decided to shower. As I stepped through to the hygiene unit, I saw myself reflected in the mirror. The hard light wasn't kind. What I saw clashed with what I remembered of myself. I had been young once, handsome even. Now grey flesh hung hollow in my cheeks, a rheumy eye peered out, the other a green, glowing orb in a metal socket. My hair was gone and my scalp was a criss-cross of scars and wires.

It hit me suddenly and one choking sob escaped me. I pitied myself for that fleeting second and then stopped.

I looked around nervously in case the central operating system had heard me, for it would send in the auto-meds to drag me off for more procedures or mind fixing drugs. I had to control my depression or my life would sink to even lower levels of misery, to one of drugged dependence, where thoughts died before they were born. Those machines never left me in peace, never let me die.

Stan's voice emerged from my mind, an unbidden memory out of the fractured puzzle of my brain, as I poured mouthwash.

'Devlin, will you stay and guard the Sinastic continent?' Stan's ruddy face, contrasted with his pale blue uniform. The background of the memory was a haze of nothingness. 'The other continent cannot be rehabilitated.

It's dead. Halfen's ecological balance is fragile. We must ensure that the balance is not disturbed...'

'We?' I muttered to myself. I had a vision of Stan and Sal. The mouthwash dispenser buckled in my fist.

Later, I descended the stairs to my ship, my one-man sky skimmer and climbed in. I set it to hover above the landing platform that jutted out like a metallic tongue above the plains of Tuemy. I wanted to take my time. It was all so pointless.

The nose lifted and I headed for the other side of the planet. All around me, dead, brown plains spread out, a symptom of decay, of human intervention.

'You...' said Other. My skin prickled everywhere. Its tone was short, elevated, urgent. I blinked, amazed at the change I could detect.

'Other?' I asked, searching for a sign of it, as I always did, since the time it first spoke to me. In the beginning, I thought it was a delusion, but the auto-meds didn't detect a chemical imbalance in my brain to explain it. So I stopped wondering after awhile and accepted it. The Other was either me, or it was something alien, an expression of a planet shocked into being by a catastrophic event that threatened its existence.

The heaviness fractured, the presence fled. 'Other!' I called, suddenly chilled by that feeling of aloneness.

In puzzlement I turned on the ship's scanners, watching the telemetry readouts. They phased in and out. After I tapped the unit, the readout stabilised. I stared at the screen. I had never seen readings like those before. It took a while for my brain to calibrate, anticipate, extrapolate...

'No...it can't be.' My voice was a thin trail of saliva trapped sound.

I accelerated, leaving a moisture trail in the upper atmosphere as I zeroed in on the co-ordinates. I watched the readouts, like a countdown.

'Other,' I whispered, but there was only silence.

As I neared my destination, I saw it, a tendril of purple, spreading out like an infection.

It was a nightmare, a reoccurring dream. I'd seen its like before, in those frigid dreams of mine. The grasping hand of death as it spread through the mousolis. It couldn't be real. I closed my tired old eye, trying to shut it out. If this was reality, then reality meant failure, failure meant meaninglessness and that meant a wasted life. My life.

I flew over, counted them. Five interlopers, five who ignored the warning buoys, five who prospected for something of value within the crust of Halfen.

I banked right, gaining altitude. Already the destruction had spread but that did not stop these beings. They couldn't see it. Their greed led them on.

I landed on a patch of desiccated ground, already darkening from their touch. I had never set foot on this continent before. I found that I couldn't now.

Fear and self-loathing held my foot immobile. Trembling, I had to tell myself over and over again that the damage was done, that my foot would not make a difference. But the impediment was there, the internal command to do no ill.

I felt the thick, dense presence of Other strongly here, poised in outrage. I reacted as if it was storm raging, my breath shortening, my eyes dilating, my skin throbbing.

'Other,' I choked out in a raspy whisper. The sense of Other's nearness splintered as my boot hit the ground.

I took a step. How did this happen? Dry sobs stole up my throat. They shocked me, controlled me.

Foot after foot I drew closer to the visitors. A terrible sound drifted close. At first, I thought my aural device was malfunctioning. I jiggled it, pulled at it, extracted it and shook it. Sliding it home, I heard it again. A drawn out wail that chilled the metal in my teeth implants, sending shredding vibrations into my head.

Over the rise, I trod until I saw them. Eager hands reached out, contorted bodies writhed and grasping limbs struggled. I tumbled down the rest of the slope and landed close to one of the interlopers. They were human throats that made those sounds. I tried to take in their predicament. The man closest to me was half-submerged in the soil to around mid-thigh. Terror gripped the man's throat, an unending keening that made me think my own skin was being sloughed off by it.

I crawled to the woman, helmet discarded, tears and snot trailing from her face. She had fallen sideways, the ground slicing across her hips and half her abdomen. I could only stare. She was so much like Sal, with brown hair, yellow skin and white teeth, that my body shook with recollection. I was seized by the memory of touching her with my hands and my lips. But the memory of Sal's face smiled. It wasn't stretched into that awful grimace.

I dragged myself upright, my eyes taking in the intruders all in a similar state. I hadn't sunk beneath the ground so I didn't think that it was soil instability. But why were they screaming?

I backed away, wishing that I couldn't hear, wishing I was back on the Destratic continent with Other for company.

'Other,' I called out.

No reply, but I felt its presence again, the denseness building to suffocating levels.

I scanned the area. There was nothing there but these humans. I was human.

The first man lifted his leg. I screamed, my voice joining with theirs.

A half-eaten stump of the man's leg, thumped the ground, and was sucked back in, dragging the man with it.

Then I understood. I jumped backwards. 'Other!' I called, head searching, scanner pinpointing.

'You?' I felt Other's bone crushing response.

'What is happening? I'm afraid.' My chest felt constricted. My heart felt ready to burst.

'You.' Other spoke to me, still and quiet from the centre of itself. I was conversing with the eye of a storm.

'Yes. It's me. Why are you killing them?'

'Them?' A squall of outrage buffeted me.

'Yes, them.'

I swivelled my head but there was no one else to be seen. No Other personified.

The spreading blackness of the dying mousolis etched itself onto my mind. As it spread, so did the gnawing darkness inside of me. It was if that decay was me. It represented what I truly was. 'You must not kill them,' I called to Other.

'Them?'

'Them,' I shouted, pointing towards the slowly sinking humans. The woman was chest deep, blood coughed through her pain-gripped lips.

'Them...remember them.' The heaviness roiled. I felt my head succumb to the pressure, felt my bones contract.

'Them?' I asked, though the understanding that I felt lurking chilled me.

'Yes...remember them. Remember what they did.'

I tried to back away from the dissolving humans. But my feet had sunk into the ground. I lifted a boot and the sole peeled away. The other foot sunk lower.

'Other?'

'Yes.'

'Stop. I am your friend.'

'Friend? You?

'Yes that's right. Me.'

'I remember them.'

'Yes, you remember them. They are not the same them. But it's the same me. Don't do this to me.' I was begging, fearing the death that I had so longed for.

'You,' Other called, its voice grating and deep.

'Yes...Other.'

'I remember you.'

'Me?' I screamed as I was sucked further down. Then a memory that sharpened my dull senses sprung out of me, out of my fear. Me and Sal running through the plains of Tuemy, the first feet to touch the surface. We were so filled with joy, with the open space, that we had rolled around, stripping off our ship suits to press our flesh together. I tasted her sweet mouth, smelled her musky scent and while I sowed my seed, our presence had sown the seeds of death for Halfen. Beneath our naked skin, talons of decay spread out, fanning in all directions without end.

It was me, in my haste; me, who soiled this planet with my presence. That is why I stayed. I had given myself to save the Sinastic Continent...and failed.

Author Note

This is one of my earlier stories and I can't quite remember the genesis of it. I know I liked the idea of the planet being sentient and the idea of repentance and service. Obviously, I liked the fact that Devlin failed. It is symbolic I think about standing against change and not succeeding.

Abandoned Time

In abandoned time, leaves long bled of colour cling to clawed and blackened branches and those that have fallen lay among the bare roots, rotting but never deteriorating into humus to join once again with the circle of life. Shadows caught mid-crawl are frozen and stale, like shattered moments ripe with tears that have been thrust into the past and forgotten. There are echoes of echoes here, empty whispers where all meaning has floated away, gradually decayed by time until the once sharp thoughts become fragile and faint.

I tread the land of abandoned time, at first as a tourist, though circumstance made me its prisoner. I pass under the trees with leaves frozen mid-flutter as if hushed by a small puff of God's breath. The sky is always the same, the sun neither rising nor setting, its pallid hand like a dying man's stretching grasping fingers over the horizon. Futile is the sun's attempt to break the day or bind the night, it is caught in null time's thrall.

In between time worn sandstone pathways I walk in search of he who led and left me here. My heart is slowing and soon this time, this place, will cool my blood and make my mind forget to inhale the remnants of countless exhalations and sighs.

The grove up ahead is like a fake floral arrangement left too long in the sun and whose petals are fading to sepia and turning up at the edges. It fascinates me and I hurry to it, though my breath burns in my throat. My heart is beating with a painful fractured drum.

There among the crispy autumn leaves with the last vestiges of colour painted along their veins he lies. His face is pale in the moment of death, but I see that perhaps he is not dead at all, but hovering on the cusp of it, waiting for the one who loves him to forget the strong line of his jaw, the fond contours of his widow's peak and the slightly crooked teeth which often graced his smile. Farther on, I see the dried bones of former travellers, who perhaps entered here long ago and the memory of them has passed out of existence as time elsewhere moved on.

My gaze now is tinged with red. My time is ending, as the shunned memories of eons press against me. I lay down beside him, rest my head on his still chest and listen as my heart slows and my blood congeals, as the air whispers from my lungs never to return. And then as I am forgotten, as my deeds have been swept away by the gentle winds of time, I will decompose into the leaf mulch that never stirs in the wind, that never completely rots, but is abandoned and forgotten for all time.

Author Note

This idea for a flash fiction piece came to me listening to an Italian folk singer. He sings about il tempo abandnado – Abandoned Time - well that's how I heard it and I thought about how this could be. A place where time has leaked away and I conceived it then of a place where time travellers can become trapped and, as the universe forgets them, they slowly fade as if they never were.

Publication History

'Beneath the Floating City' was first published in *Anywhere But Earth*, 2011, coeur de lion.

'Green, Green Grass of Homeworld' was published in *Belong*, 2010, Ticonderoga.

'Night of Masks and Spears, was published in *Masques*, 2009, CSFG Publishing.

'Warning Buoy' was published in *Deep Space Terror*, 2010, Static Movement.

'Lake Absence' has not been published previously.

'Other' was published in *Elsewhere*, 2003, CSFG Publishing.

'Abandoned Time' was published in *Flashspec Vol 2*, 2007, Equilibrium Books

About Donna Maree Hanson

Donna Maree Hanson is a traditionally and independently published author of fantasy, science fiction and horror. She also writes paranormal romance under the pseudonym of Dani Kristoff. Her dark fantasy series (which some reviewers have called 'grim dark'), Dragon Wine, was published by Momentum Books (Pan Macmillan digital imprint). Part one: *Shatterwing* and Part two, *Skywatcher* are out now in digital and print on demand along with two new instalments, *Deathwings, Part three* and *Bloodstorm, part four*. The four Dragon Wine books are available in ebook and print.

In April 2015, she was awarded the A. Bertram Chandler Award for 'Outstanding Achievement in Australian Science Fiction' for her work in running science fiction conventions, publishing and broader SF community contribution.

Donna also writes young adult science fiction, with *Rayessa and the Space Pirates* and *Rae and Essa's Space Adventures* out with Escape Publishing. *Opi Battles the Space Pirates* was published independently in 2017.

Her first Indie published book, *Argenterra*, was published in late April 2016. *Argenterra* is the first in an epic fantasy series (the Silverlands) suitable for adult and young adult readers. *Oathbound* and *Ungiven Land* complete the series and these are available in ebook book and print.

In 2016, Donna commenced her PhD candidature researching feminism in popular romance at the University of Canberra. Donna lives in Canberra with her partner and fellow writer Matthew Farrer.

If you want to hear more from Donna and about new work sign up to her newsletter.

Newsletter sign up form.

Donna Maree Hanson's Books

Love and Space Pirates series (science fiction romance)

Rayessa and the Space Pirates

Rae and Essa's Space Adventures

Opi Battles the Space Pirates

Dragon Wine series (dark fantasy)

Shatterwing

Skywatcher

Deathwings

Bloodstorm

Skyfire (due 2018)

Moonfall (due 2018)

Silverlands series (epic fantasy)

Argenterra

Oathbound

Ungiven Land